ABSOLUTE THREAT

(A JAKE MERCER POLITICAL THRILLER—BOOK 1)

JACK MARS

Jack Mars

Jack Mars is the USA Today bestselling author of the LUKE STONE thriller series, which includes seven books. He is also the author of the new FORGING OF LUKE STONE prequel series, comprising six books; of the AGENT ZERO spy thriller series, comprising twelve books; of the TROY STARK thriller series, comprising seven books; of the SPY GAME thriller series, comprising nine books; and of the new JAKE MERCER thriller series, comprising five books (and counting).

Jack loves to hear from you, so please feel free to visit www.Jackmarsauthor.com to join the email list, receive a free book, receive free giveaways, connect on Facebook and Twitter, and stay in touch!

ISBN: 978-1-0943-9696-5

BOOKS BY JACK MARS

JAKE MERCER THRILLER SERIES
ABSOLUTE THREAT (Book #1)
ABSOLUTE DAMAGE (Book #2)
ABSOLUTE FORCE (Book #3)
ABSOLUTE PERIL (Book #4)
ABSOLUTE TREASON (Book #5)

THE SPY GAME
TARGET ONE (Book #1)
TARGET TWO (Book #2)
TARGET THREE (Book #3)
TARGET FOUR (Book #4)
TARGET FIVE (Book #5)
TARGET SIX (Book #6)
TARGET SEVEN (Book #7)
TARGET EIGHT (Book #8)

TROY STARK THRILLER SERIES
ROGUE FORCE (Book #1)
ROGUE COMMAND (Book #2)
ROGUE TARGET (Book #3)
ROGUE MISSION (Book #4)
ROGUE SHOT (Book #5)
ROGUE STRIKE (Book #6)
ROGUE ORDER (Book #7)

LUKE STONE THRILLER SERIES
ANY MEANS NECESSARY (Book #1)
OATH OF OFFICE (Book #2)
SITUATION ROOM (Book #3)
OPPOSE ANY FOE (Book #4)
PRESIDENT ELECT (Book #5)
OUR SACRED HONOR (Book #6)
HOUSE DIVIDED (Book #7)

FORGING OF LUKE STONE PREQUEL SERIES

PRIMARY TARGET (Book #1)
PRIMARY COMMAND (Book #2)
PRIMARY THREAT (Book #3)
PRIMARY GLORY (Book #4)
PRIMARY VALOR (Book #5)
PRIMARY DUTY (Book #6)

AN AGENT ZERO SPY THRILLER SERIES

AGENT ZERO (Book #1)
TARGET ZERO (Book #2)
HUNTING ZERO (Book #3)
TRAPPING ZERO (Book #4)
FILE ZERO (Book #5)
RECALL ZERO (Book #6)
ASSASSIN ZERO (Book #7)
DECOY ZERO (Book #8)
CHASING ZERO (Book #9)
VENGEANCE ZERO (Book #10)
ZERO ZERO (Book #11)
ABSOLUTE ZERO (Book #12)

PROLOGUE

The scene reminded Jake Mercer of those overly enthusiastic period musicals from the 1940s that his grandmother used to love. In those movies, Small Town America always bustled with excitement on Independence Day. Couples walked arm in arm, the men donning red, white, and blue top hats. Children ran to and fro carrying patriotic pinwheels. In the background, a brass band played John Phillip Sousa or Woody Guthrie or some other icon of Parlophone folk. Every town in those musicals had a brass band and at least two dozen curly-haired cherubic faced blondes prancing around in clothing that for the time was almost shockingly risqué.

There was nothing small about the Lincoln Memorial, but the patriotism on display was exactly the sort one might find even today in Small Town America.

The sights and the thoughts came to him in an instant, but he couldn't dwell on them. He was too busy looking for inconsistencies, things that didn't fit. The scowling man with his arms crossed staring defiantly at the flag while others saluted it. The woman with the flat expression gazing with a little too much interest at the security detail surrounding the President. The young men wearing hoodies emblazoned with the logo of whatever anti-government movement was popular these days.

Inconsistencies could be threats, and finding those threats and stopping them before they became dangers was his job.

The President of the United States stood at the foot of the monument stairs wearing his storied smile. He wasn't the first president Jake had served, but he had spent a great deal of his time close to this man, and he recognized the practiced kindness sprinkled with gravity in the President's smile. Not that it wasn't genuine. A surprising number of politicians were very genuine in their beliefs. They were just better at controlling their emotions and articulating their points of view than the average citizen.

Of course, quite a few of them had no control over their emotions and couldn't articulate the back of a cereal box even if they had an English professor helping them. But President Bryan Jackson was not one of those politicians. As he smiled at the crowd, Jake could see the smile working its magic. Bryan accomplished the magical balance between distant, important, gravitas-filled leader and compassionate, approachable everyman. Even if it seemed to Jake a practiced and carefully manicured skill, he couldn't help but admire it.

Something was wrong.

He scanned the crowd, but he saw nothing that seemed out of the ordinary. The crowd continued to cheer and wave their flags. He sniffed the air but smelled only the crispness of the late winter.

Then he heard it: a soft ticking sound that just barely reached his eardrums.

There was no mistaking what that sound was."Get him out of here!" he hissed into his mouthpiece, as he rushed toward the President. He was halfway there before he heard the explosion, followed by the screams. He wanted to look back, but he didn't. Not yet. First, he needed to get the President to safety.

The acrid smell of explosives reached his nose, mingled with the screams of those who were dying.

Images flashed in his mind. He refused to acknowledge them for fear they would overwhelm him. The smoke and the screams made bile rise in his throat and he fought an urge to vomit.

He reached the President, and everything snapped into focus. In moments like these, Jake felt more like a machine than a man. He was a tool, and like all tools, he would serve his purpose.

At the moment, his purpose was to get the President to safety. He and his team surrounded Bryan and led him quickly to the waiting armored van.

With the President heading where he needed to, Jake turned around and scanned the scene behind him.

The front steps of the Memorial had been blown to rubble. Bodies lay strewn across the steps. Some of them still moved and cried out. Some of them didn't.

The screams of the injured were bad. The silence of those who couldn't scream anymore were worse.

He pushed those images to the side and looked for the attackers. A flash of movement caught the corner of his eye, and he turned and saw a man in a balaclava raise a handgun to aim at the President. Jake leveled his own handgun and fired faster than the attacker could pull the trigger. The round severed the attacker's brainstem, and he fell to the ground in a heap, the connection between his body and brain instantly destroyed.

Through the crowd, he could see other attackers fleeing, but even with his immaculate aim, there was too much risk of hitting a civilian for him to try another shot.

"Five men, armed and dangerous, heading east of the memorial," he said. "All wearing balaclavas, all of medium build, dark windbreakers."

With that said, he turned to the President and helped him into the limo. There was nothing else he could do to stop the attackers right now. His mission was to protect the President of the United States. It would be up to others to find the perpetrators.

***

One hour later, Jake returned to the scene. The President was safe in Outpost Alpha and would remain there until Jake said otherwise. Before Jake could authorize his return to the White House, he needed to have an understanding of the threat. Was this a simple assassination attempt or a terrorist plot?

He showed his ID to the Capitol Police officer protecting the scene, then walked through the yellow tape and approached a detective talking to another uniform. The detective looked irritated to see him, and that expression didn't change when Jake showed him his Secret Service ID.

"Can I help you, Agent?"

Jake would never understand why people thought he would get all bent out of shape out of having the word "Special" dropped from his title. Why was everyone so damned petty anyway?

"Do you have any preliminary reports on the attackers?"

"My office will send a full report to the President's security detail when we have information."

Jake simply stared in reply. In his experience, most people who knew they were in the wrong would eventually break if you just made eye contact long enough.

This detective was no exception. After a moment, he sighed and said, "We don't know, but we found this on the body of the assailant who was killed."

He reached into his pocket and pulled out an evidence bag. Inside the bag was a single scrap of paper with one word written on it.

RETRIBUTION.

CHAPTER ONE

Jake met the detective's eyes. "See, this is something we need to know right away, detective."

"You'll have my full—"

"Fuck your full report. These assholes just killed a bunch of people and tried to kill the President. You find evidence, it comes to me before it goes anywhere else. In fact, if I see a report from you or anyone else that has anything written in it that you haven't already told me, I'm going to make it my mission in life to make sure your next job is shoveling gorilla shit at the National Zoo. You got me?"

The detective's smarmy attitude vanished. He swallowed and said in a shaky voice, "Yes, sir."

"Outstanding."

He turned and left the pale, shaking detective and moved ahead to examine the scene.

This wasn't the first time Jake had felt angry. He ran a little hotter than most agents, although usually, he was able to keep that heat under control. He most certainly ran hot when it came to attacks on U.S. soil. He ran hot enough to be scorching when it came to attacks that threatened the President of the United States. In the Secret Service, there were celebrated agents who seemed almost robotic in their ability to maintain complete, cold indifference. Jake didn't understand them, unless maybe they were just as angry as he was and just better at hiding it.

Well, Jake didn't feel like a robot at the moment, and he wasn't interested in projecting cold indifference. Right now, Jake felt like murder. Right now, Jake felt like there were very few things he could imagine wanting more than revenge.

Retribution.

For what? For fuck's sake, Bryan was loved by both parties! Well, relatively speaking, anyway. He had won the Presidency by managing to appease opposing viewpoints and then actually acting in a bipartisan manner in office. Hell, the opposing party's majority leader had thrown him a surprise birthday party the year before.

He would give anything to have the people responsible for this attack standing in front of him right now.

Of course, if they were in front of him, he'd process them like any suspects, but fantasizing about taking justice into his own hands took the edge off and allowed him to focus on his job. It made it a little easier for him to deal with the situation, with the half-dozen mounds on the lawn covered with sheets and marked with flags

"How are we looking, Jake?"

Jess Foster, Jake's partner, was his polar opposite in almost every way. Young, bubbly and almost painfully optimistic, she spoke now with the same breezy cheer that always colored her voice.

The one thing that they had in common was an unfailing work ethic and commitment to their mission. That was why Jake could handle her indomitable joy. He tapped his earpiece and said, "It's a zoo. As usual."

There were, of course, investigators from just about every imaginable law enforcement agency. The Capitol Police, represented by Detective Fuckwad, would want their day in the sun. The FBI would get involved because of the terrorist nature of the attack. The Washington, DC, Police would scramble for jurisdiction as always. Since the attack took place on government ground, they had the least claim, but the current mayor and, therefore, police department were in favor with the current Congress, so they would get some spotlight as well.

Strictly speaking, this investigation belonged to the National Park Service. Anything that ever happened on the National Mall belonged to the National Park Service, although Jake doubted like hell the National Park Service would want to touch this with a fifty-foot pole.

But an attack on the President always trumped everything else. So, this was a Secret Service investigation regardless of what other agencies were involved.

There would still be posturing. Polite people would call it jockeying for position. Others, less polite, would talk about measuring anatomy. Ultimately, though, there was only one agency in charge here, and it was the Secret Service.

"Sounds about right. Look around the scene and see what you can find. Try to remember that the zoo animals don't know any better."

He chuckled and said, "If that were true, then I wouldn't be angry."

"Still, let's not earn ourselves another lecture. If I fall asleep in front of Arthur again, I'm going to end up working a reception desk, and then where will you be?"

"All right," he said, "I'll keep myself calm."

"Good boy."

He surveyed the area and tried to keep the anger at bay. Technicians were mapping the direction of the crowds' movements during the attack. The arrows they laid down would be used to establish a timeline relevant to crowd behavior. If they were lucky, it might tell them where the attackers came from and possibly help them identify the assailants.

"Jess, we've got Capitol Police CSI tracking crowd movements. Have you been in contact with them yet?"

One of Jess's many valuable qualities was her connection to nearly every agency in D.C. and the surrounding areas. How she had managed to develop such a network at only twenty-five years old was beyond Jake, but he was very grateful for it.

"They've sent me the footage they have."

"And?"

"It's a lot. There were over fifty thousand people attending that event. Figuring out exactly who attacked the President is either going to be very easy or nearly impossible."

"Wonderful. Anything we can do to make it tend to very easy and not nearly impossible?"

"I'm looking at the attack and working backwards. I've traced the men who fired on the President back to five minutes before the President arrived."

"Five minutes? That's it?"

"Like I said, it's a lot of footage, and their behavior only changed in the moments leading to the attack."

"But they wore balaclavas."

"They did for the few minutes leading up to the attack, but they didn't wear them at first."

"That seems risky."

"Attempting to assassinate the President seems risky."

"Fair enough. So do we have faces?"

"The most generic everyman faces you could possibly think of. These guys were born to get away with murder."

"Well, let's make sure they don't."

"Obviously, Jake. I was just using a figure of speech."

Jake took one last look around the scene and decided he wasn't going to get anything else snooping around. "I'm going to get some coffee. You want me to bring you anything?"

"Ooh! I want a caramel macchiato with whipped cream and oat milk, please?"

Jake grimaced. "Oat milk? How the hell do you milk an oat?"

“You ask really nicely and don’t skimp on the foreplay.”

“Thanks,” he replied drily. “I needed that image.”

“Welcome!”

“At the risk of making you even more annoying than you already are, have you ever considered drinking coffee?”

“That is coffee! They make it with espresso!”

“They make tiramisu with espresso too.”

She sighed. “Okay, grumpy Gus. How about you get yourself the blackest, strongest coffee you can find and drink the whole thing before you get here so I don’t have to deal with Ralph Kramden all day.”

“Who’s Ralph Kramden?”

“Seriously? You’ve never seen the Honeymooners?”

He rolled his eyes but noticed that he was smiling too. “I’ll get your sugar sprinkled with coffee.”

“I mean it. Lotta coffee. Drink it on your way here.”

***

Despite the importance of the agency, Secret Service Headquarters was typically a rather calm place. There hadn’t been a serious attempt on a U.S. President’s life in forty years, and with the sophisticated detection technologies in existence today, the agency’s second mission of hunting counterfeiters was a far cry from what it used to be.

It was a testament to the seriousness of the situation that the headquarters now looked like a stock exchange in peak trading hour. Agents bustled to and fro, talking over phones and into radios. Grim looks and anxious speech filled that air.

Jake navigated through this cacophony until he reached the office that his partner used. Jess sat at the computer scrolling through footage of the attack. She smiled and waved happily when Jake walked in.

Some things never change, Jake thought wryly.

He handed Jess her liquid ice cream and sipped a brew that was indeed as black and bitter as he could wish. “I looked up Ralph Kramden while I was waiting for my coffee,” he told her. “Fuck you.”

Jess grinned at him, full lips parting underneath hazel eyes that seemed to glow underneath auburn hair that framed her face in delicate waves. She was beautiful. Though Jake had no intention of acting on that, he couldn’t help but notice how attractive she was. He noted the fact almost with surprise. It seemed to him, as much as anything else, that she seemed far too competent to also be so damned attractive.

“You’re sweet, but I like nice guys. Here, check this out.”

Another thing Jake appreciated about Jess was her ability to instantly switch off the banter when the situation called for seriousness. Her cheerfulness remained, but her eyes carried an intensity that Jake thought might be the most attractive thing about her.

Not that he was attracted to her. In another life, he might allow himself to feel that way, but she was his partner, and he wouldn't allow himself to feel that way about his partner.

"So, our gentleman are, as we've discussed earlier, average Joe looking guys. Late twenties to late thirties, which makes them a little old for the anti-government type, but exceptions prove the rule, as they say."

She pointed out four men seen mingling with the crowd. Jake checked the timestamp and saw that it was fifteen minutes before the speech. They were, as Jess said, average Joe looking types. Even their facial expressions seemed benign. These guys were professionals.

"Back this up about twenty minutes," Jess said, pressing a button on her computer, "And the Wonderbread Boys are seen getting out of this van."

The van in question was a passenger van that looked as generic as the assailants. It was an older model but not too old, maybe fifteen years or so, old enough to still be based on a sturdy truck frame and have a powerful V-8 engine but new enough that it wouldn't look out of place among the other cars parked nearby.

"Do we have a plate?"

"Not yet."

"See if you can find one."

Jess gave him a frank look, and he lifted his hands placatingly and said, "Okay. *When* you find the plate that you're already looking for, give it to Washington PD and tell them to call us when they find it."

"Will do. That'll give them a reason to feel important too."

"It'll make them actually important, which is even better. The more we can demonstrate cooperation, the more other agencies will be willing to cooperate."

"You really think so?"

"Well…" he let the subject drop and said, "Hold on. Go back a bit."

"What? Did you see something?"

"I think so. Go back to when they get out of the van."

She did, and when Jake saw it again, he said, "Go back one frame at a time."

Jess did, and Jake stopped her again when he saw the flash of skin just above one of the men's ankles as he stepped out of the van. "There. Can you enhance that image?"

Jess zoomed in on the tiny square of image at the bottom of the picture. There was a limit to how much she could enhance the image, but it was enough to make it clear what the tattoo on the man's ankle was.

A three-pronged trident in a circle with a halo above the prongs. The prongs stood for Liberty, Justice and Prosperity. A rather innocuous name for a group whose MO was to cause violent riots and use terrorism to advocate for their message of anarchy.

"Trident," Jess whispered.

"Looks like they've graduated from causing a ruckus to killing people," Jake said, his lighthearted tone masking his anger.

Jess, for once, was at a loss for words. She turned back to the screen, her lips pressed tightly together.

Trident was on Homeland Security's terrorism watchlist. That meant they were on the Secret Service's watchlist too, along with those of the FBI, the CIA and the NSA. Despite this, no one had really taken them seriously.

It looked like that was about to change.

Jake's cell phone rang. He answered, and Detective Fuckwad of the Capitol Police Department said, "Hello, Special Agent. It's Detective Brown."

He remembered the Special part this time, Jake thought. *How nice.*

"What do you have for me, Detective?"

"An address. We found a cell phone on the body of the deceased assailant. Most of the data is corrupted, but we were able to get an address. A partial one, anyway."

"Send it to me."

"Will do."

Jake hung up and stood. "I'm going to check out an address that Capitol PD has for me. If you get anything else from the video, let me know."

"I will. Be careful, Jake."

Jake thought of explaining to her that nothing he could possibly encounter here would be even remotely as dangerous as what he had seen overseas, but instead, he only nodded. "I will."

He made it three steps before his phone buzzed again. His boss, Arthur Davis, Director of the Secret Service. "Mercer," he answered.

"Jake, I need you in my office, ASAP."

"Can it wait? I have an address possibly connected to the assailants."

"It can't wait. Sorry, Jake."

Jake sighed. "No problem, sir. I'll be right there."

"Art?" Jess asked when Jake hung up.

"Yep."

"Then you *really* need to be careful."

"Nah. He likes me."

"Lucky you," Jess said drily.

"He likes you too. You just annoy him sometimes."

"Gee, thanks partner."

"Welcome!" he said, mimicking her cheery voice.

She stuck her tongue out at him, and he chuckled as he left the room.

CHAPTER TWO

Jack noted that Arthur Davis's office reflected the man's personality. It seemed a mirror of his nature in more ways than one. At the moment, that was illustrated by the fact that the office was impeccably clean, impeccably organized, and impeccably maintained. If the Director could be summed up in one word, impeccable would be that word.

"Have a seat, Jack," Art said in his typical, gruff voice.

Jack moved quickly to obey, taking a seat in one of two wooden guest chairs in front of Davis's desk. The chair was, like Davis, impeccable. It was high quality, developed with old American craftsmanship. It wasn't simplistic by any means, but it was, nonetheless, simple and understandable. There was no pretense in the chair, no pretense in the office, and no pretense in Arthur Davis.

"Jake," Art said, "reality and fantasy are different."

"Yes, Sir," Jake said. He had no idea where Art intended to go with that comment but *Yes, Sir* was always a safe response.

"Did you want to be Carlos Hathcock?"

Carlos Hathcock was a sniper. *The* sniper. Most people with more than a passing interest in the military knew about Hathcock. These days, people really only knew about snipers from Hollywood movies. "I suppose every Marine with a rifle wanted to be Carlos Hathcock, Sir," he replied.

"But especially snipers."

"Yes, Sir."

"Do you think Hathcock would have followed orders he found distasteful?"

Jake considered his words carefully. "I believe any Marine worth his rifle would follow orders he finds distasteful, Sir," he said, a trifle thinly.

Art smiled. "Yes. Yes, you're right. So, let me ask you. Do you think Hathcock would have followed orders he believed to be illegal or deadly to the lives of his brothers and sisters in arms?"

"I believe Hathcock was a hell of a shot, Sir," Jake said.

Art chuckled and said, “You don’t like the dance. Okay. I can respect that. Jake, you directly disobeyed orders in the middle of combat and in the process won the bronze star for saving the lives of more than a dozen Marines. Anyone with a head on his shoulders sees you as an asset. Some short-sighted individuals focused more on the chain of command than the quality of command might see things differently. They’re wrong.”

Jake said nothing. He didn’t know where Art was taking this, and under the circumstances, he didn’t want to try to guess. “Jake, you have a code of ethics and honor that informs your code of conduct. You make decisions based on what you believe is right and not based on what you’re told is expedient.”

Jake wasn’t sure if Art intended that as a compliment, so he only nodded slightly in response.

“Your career in the Marine Corps was decorated and impressive,” Art said, “and the truth is, it’s a liability to you rather than an asset. That isn’t fair but it’s reality. You’re not celebrated for it even though the ribbons and medals might suggest you should be.”

Finally, Jake couldn’t wait any longer. “May I ask where you’re going with this, sir?”

“The fact is, Jake, that most agencies are going to see this as a political opportunity. Everyone wants to be the agency responsible for solving the case. That matters more to most than making sure there are no further assaults on the President and no more dead third graders. That’s not the case with this agency, and it’s not the case with you.”

“No, sir.”

“And that’s why I’m making you lead on this investigation.”

Jake blinked. “Investigation, sir?”

“That shouldn’t come as a surprise to you. You’ve been investigating nonstop since this event occurred.”

“Yes, sir, to determine the risk of another attack on the President.”

“And now your scope of responsibility includes bringing these assassins to justice.”

Jake tried to hide his discomfort and kept his tone even as he said, “With all due respect, Sir, aren’t we exceeding our prerogative if we do that?”

“We’ve already exceeded it, and we’ll continue to exceed it. As long as exceeding it is what we need to do to ensure the President is kept safe. I don’t intend to be passive here, Jake. Our job is the safety of the President of the United States and his family, and that’s more than just being a bodyguard. We need to address each and every threat the President faces, and that means we need to address this. And quite frankly, I don't see any other agency doing as good of a job as you will do.

"You'll need to cooperate with those agencies, of course. Jess has a lot of connections. Use them. But *you* are in charge, and it will be up to you to remind people of that fact."

"I'll do my best, sir."

"You'll succeed," Art retorted.

"I'm a Marine, sir," Jake said. "Those two phrases mean the same thing to me."

Art cracked a smile. "Wonderful. Use whatever resources you need. I'll approve them, and if you need another agency's resources, and they give you trouble, I'll make sure they suffer greatly for it."

Jake stood and extended his hand. "Thank you, sir."

"Don't thank me. Just do your job."

He shook Jake's hand anyway, though. "Good luck, Special Agent."

Jake left the office and headed toward the break room. He needed a moment to think through his situation. It wasn't as simple as going to the address and gleaning information anymore. He needed to know what the endgame was and how to stop it.

He made a phone call to Special Agent Grady, an FBI liaison to the Secret Service. Grady agreed to send a team of agents to check the place out and report back to Jake what they found.

Jake wished he could be out in the field himself, but that wasn't the Secret Service's responsibility. The best he could do was wait.

God, he hated waiting.

He sat at a table in the break room and leaned forward, planting his elbows on the table and steepling his fingers.

Images flashed through his mind again, and this time, they lingered.

The screams wouldn't stop. Christ, why won't they shut the fuck up?

"Mercer! Proceed to Point Charlie and wait for extraction!"

"Negative, sir. There's a squad down there in need of help."

"We have air support on the way. Get your ass to Charlie now!"

Jake looked down at the squad of Marines. Three of the Marines were injured, but all three still held their rifles and fired at the slowly closing circle of enemy combatants. Air support was on its way, but it wouldn't make it in time, and even if it did, it would be unable to engage the enemy for risk of destroying their own forces.

"Negative, sir. They won't make it in time. I'm going in."

"Mercer, Goddammit!"

"We don't leave Marines behind, sir."

He cut the comm and rushed downward. All around him, he could hear the screams of the dead and dying. All of them were enemies, but they were also people. God, why wouldn't they stop screaming?

"Jake?"

He started and looked up to see Jess standing over him, looking concerned. "Hey, Jess. Just taking a moment to gather my thoughts."

"The nightmares again?"

"Well, I'm not asleep right now, so no."

She crossed her arms and looked at him frankly. He sighed and said, "Yeah, the same thing as the nightmares, anyway."

"When are you going to get help for that?"

"When I'm dead."

"That's not funny."

"I wasn't joking. Art wants us to lead the investigation."

"Isn't that what we're already doing?"

"He wants us to lead the *full* investigation. He wants us to catch these guys, not just determine if and when they're going to attack again.

"Can he do that? Doesn't National Park Service have jurisdiction?"

"We can make ourselves have jurisdiction, and it looks like that's what he wants us to do. We'll be working with other agencies, though."

"Sounds fun."

"Sounds godawful."

"Do you need more coffee?"

He shrugged. "I think I'm good at what I do, but I don't think I'm good at leading a team."

She frowned at him, and he found it both endearing and irritating that she still looked happy. "I could spend all day telling you why you're wrong about that, but I know you won't listen, so instead, I'm going to say that you don't necessarily need to lead a team. You and I need to solve this case and use other agencies as resources when necessary. Think of the other guys as tools, not partners, and you'll have an easier time dealing with this."

"Wow. That's a lot more brutal than I would have expected from you."

"It's practical," she countered. "And they'll understand it. Even the ones that act like they don't will understand it. Get them to comply, like the detective from Capitol Police. They don't need to like you, they just need to do what you say."

He grinned at her. "You sound like my Drill Instructor."

"He sounds like a wise man."

"A woman, actually. Gunnery Sergeant Melinda Carter. Built like a brick and mean as a badger. God, I loved that woman."

"When this is over, I'll ask her out for you," she quipped.

"Jake?" Art's voice called. "I need you. Jess, you come too."

Jake turned to see his boss leaning into the break room. The others present looked at Jake and Jess with the same expressions Jake saw on recruits who just saw another recruit mouth off to a Drill Instructor. They clearly believed that Jake and Jess were about to get new holes torn on their body.

Give it time, Jake thought glumly.

He and Jess made their way to Art's office, and Jake noticed that Jess was far more subdued around Art than she was when they were alone. Art had that effect on people. Jake suppressed a smile when it occurred to him that it wasn't all that unlike Gunny Sergeant Carter's effect on people.

Art spoke without preamble. "I just received this email," he said.

He turned his computer monitor so the two of them could see it. The email was short and came from a temporary address. The subject line was RETRIBUTION.

The email read, *The first time, innocents died due to your blindness and the Fascist Emperor's cowardice. Next time, allow us our justice, or more will needlessly suffer.*

There was no signature at the bottom. Jake leaned back and said, "Well, we know there's going to be another attack now."

"Yes. I've already told the President that he is to remain at Outpost Alpha until further notice. He's unhappy, of course, but he'll comply."

"Has his family been moved yet?"

"Yes. They're at the Outpost."

"Wonderful."

"The Fascist Emperor," Jess repeated. "How colorful."

"And they're clearly not above killing civilians to get their way," Jake said.

"You see why I need you in charge of this?" Art asked.

Jake and Jess shared a look. Then Jake sighed and said, "Send the letter to Jess, please. She might be able to track it to the sender. We'll get these guys, sir."

"I know you will, Jake. Sooner rather than later would be nice."

"Yes," Jake agreed. "It would."

But as Jake knew, what would be nice very rarely aligned with reality.

CHAPTER THREE

The room shown on the screen wasn't actually a room. It was in a room, but it was nothing more than a façade. A stage. The camera would not pan from its direct shot. The carefully created sight of the president in front of a nondescript wall with vaguely patriotic art would remain unchanging. The desk in front of him appeared functional. The papers on the desk appeared functional. The phone on the desk appeared functional. None of it appeared quite worthy of the President of the United States.

Of course, it didn't.

This was the President of the United States operating in the midst of a crisis. This wasn't about pomp and circumstance. This was the Commander in Chief in the midst of his command.

Jake would ordinarily scoff at a charade like this, but he understood its necessity now. One of the President's most important roles was to offer reassurance at times like these. Part of that involved theatrics. It couldn't be helped.

Jake watched the President speak from Outpost Alpha's operations center. The operations center was actually located directly behind the façade of an American flag, the seal of the Presidency and a closeup of the chalice Lady Liberty held. Behind the camera were four Secret Service agents, but anyone who saw them would be forgiven for mistaking them as soldiers since they wore body armor instead of suits and carried MP5 carbines instead of handguns. The Outpost itself was forty feet underground and hardened against anything short of a nuclear weapon. There were seven such outposts, and three of them actually *were* hardened against nuclear weapons, but as dangerous as Trident was, they didn't have *that* kind of firepower.

Jake watched Bryan's carefully constructed facial expressions and listened to his just as carefully determined tones and enunciations with a slight frown. He respected the President a great deal, and not just the office. Bryan was, in a great many ways, far more commendable than most politicians.

Still, it grated on him how carefully manicured these speeches were, all the more because he knew that Bryan was sincere. Actually, that sincerity probably contributed to the charade. The President understood, more than most, the value of reassurance in leadership.

It just bugged Jake that people needed this fakeness to be reassured. It didn't give him a high opinion of the nation's future.

He turned his attention from the video feed and examined the standard camera feeds for any threats, starting with the rooms surrounding the President and moving to those aboveground. This safe, undisclosed location was within walking distance of the oval office. The President wouldn't have to step into the open even once to get there, either. Outposts Alpha through Delta were all located in D.C. and linked to the White House via tunnels.

Right now, there were no immediate threats. The chances of anything threatening happening to the President in this room was almost nonexistent, but he looked anyway. If nothing else, constantly scanning for threats quieted the turmoil in his mind.

He glanced at Jess, who was, like Jake, monitoring a half-dozen different screens. While his were focused entirely on the President's immediate security, hers were split between different social media platforms and camera feeds from different agencies investigating possible targets for Trident's next attack.

Jake couldn't really give a rat's ass about what the public thought of the President's speech, but watching social media was important. Many would-be assassins and terrorists had revealed themselves through social media, and if they were lucky, their killers might do the same here.

As far as the other targets, Jake had to admit that law enforcement had its uses. If there was one thing every police force in America did well, it was saturating a place with so many uniforms that a flea wouldn't get in without a permit and a strip search.

He only wished the investigative talents of other agencies were up to the same standard. The FBI had raided the address found on the dead Trident assassin's cell phone but had found nothing useful. It could very well be that there was nothing useful to be found, but Jake couldn't help but wonder if he would have found something if he looked himself.

Well, it didn't matter. He couldn't look. Regardless of his role in this investigation, his first and foremost responsibility was the protection of the President of the United States, and Bryan had requested personally that Jake handle security for this speech.

"Mackay, take over on the monitors," Jake said to one of the other agents.

Mackay slid into Jake's seat without question and without hesitation. Another thing Jake loved about the Secret Service was the military nature of the Agency. Orders were to be followed, not questioned or talked about.

Jake recognized the hypocrisy in that belief, but he was wrestling with too much right now to dwell on it. He walked over to Jess and said, "I'd offer you a cup of coffee, but I see that you won't drink it."

"I keep telling you to install cappuccino makers in these Outposts," she retorted. "I can't drink dirt water the way you can."

"You mean espresso makers."

"I mean the things that make good tasting drinks and not tea made out of ground up fruit pits."

"Because tea made from leaves is so much better."

"I didn't say that. You know, you guys would benefit from a little something sweet in your life, anyway. Would it kill you to add a little sugar to your coffee?"

"I'd be just fine. Can't say the same for whatever poor soul decides to put sugar in my coffee."

She rolled her eyes. "God, no wonder you're single."

Jake chuckled and pointed at the screen. "Got anything for me?"

"Once again, far more than enough. You remember that algorithm I created a while back that flags potentially suspicious social media posts?"

"I remember."

"Well, here are all the posts that are suspicious."

She clicked an icon and nearly half of the posts highlighted red. "Christ," Jake swore. "All of this?"

"All of it."

Jake sighed. "Would you kill me if I asked if the algorithm you're using isn't discerning enough?"

"No, but I'd throw my coffee in your face. It's cold now, so it won't burn you, but your clothes will smell like coffee all day."

"Sounds unpleasant."

"I mean it. I'll mildly irritate you if you talk shit on my algorithm."

"So why so many suspicious posts?"

"Well," she said, clicking a couple more buttons. "Part of it is the fact that not many people are talking about this."

Jake's eyes widened. "Seriously? A terrorist attack kills six people and nearly kills the president and people don't care?"

"Oh, people care," she replied. "It's pretty much the only story in the news right now. But the ones talking about it here are either ultrapatriotic types calling for an immediate airstrike on the attacker, or these guys."

She showed him a sample of the highlighted posts. Some seemed innocuous. *Hey, does the President's collar look tighter to you?* Others seemed like random ads created by bots. *He should try Karma's new royal jelly honey!* Still others seemed completely off the wall. *Make sure the hooks are lined up correctly.*

"Some sort of code?"

"I think so. I'm going to gather everything and see if I can sift through it and figure something out."

"Let me know what you find."

"Are you sure? I was planning on keeping everything entirely to myself."

He rolled his eyes. "Ha ha."

The President finished his speech, and after a moment of recording Bryan's trademark smile, the cameras cut out. Bryan's smile vanished immediately. "So that's it? I can go home now?"

"No, sir," Special Agent Aronson replied. "I'm sorry, but you and your family will need to remain here until we know it's safe."

"If I remain here, then I look like I've been driven underground. I can't hide and expect the people of the United States to rally behind me."

Jake sighed and shared a look with Jess. "I need to go handle this."

"Have fun!" she called, never taking her eyes from her monitors.

She entered the room and the President gestured toward him. "Jake, can you get me home? Please, I can't be underground. This is the wrong time to show weakness."

"This is an even worse time to die, sir," Jake replied. "I understand your frustration, but you do need to stay here. We have evidence that another attack is taking place soon."

"You can protect me at the White House."

Jake sighed and leaned closer to whisper to him. "Bryan, it's too dangerous. These guys are serious players, and they've already nearly assassinated you."

"Emphasis on nearly." The President sighed. "Jake, we *must* show strength. We can't let people start to think that terrorists can frighten the President."

"I'm more concerned with making sure they don't kill the President, sir."

Bryan pulled back and glared at Jake. Jake held his gaze, keenly aware of the discomfort the other agents felt. The Secret Service was unique in that its agents were empowered to tell the President no when the circumstances required it.

No one enjoyed when that had to happen, though. Jake might be on a first-name basis with the President, but that didn't mean he was any more comfortable with defying his wishes than anyone was.

But when the alternative was allowing him to put himself in danger, he had no trouble refusing to comply with the President's wishes. His comfort paled in comparison to his mission.

Finally, the President sighed. He shook his head and brought his thumb and forefinger to the bridge of his nose. "All right. But please keep in mind that while my safety matters, so too does the reputation of the United States government. If we send the message that any terrorist attack that occurs is going to make us scurry into holes like rabbits, then every wannabe terrorist in the world is going to be emboldened to act."

Jake frowned slightly. He had considered that very thing, and the result the President predicted was exactly what worried him.

But he had no choice. The President's safety *was* paramount, and right now, they had reason to believe that another attack would come soon if Bryan was allowed free roam.

The other agents escorted the President to his quarters. Jake sighed and headed back to the situation room. With the speech over, Mackay had gone to assist in other areas and Jess was the only one in the room.

"Got anything for me?"

"A little bit of a lot of different things, but they're all the same thing really."

Jake smiled drily. "Thank you. That clears everything up."

"I'm just as annoyed as you are," she said, "but that's really all I have. I've narrowed down the suspicious communications to six different accounts. You can see here that while all of the accounts post seemingly random stuff, they all follow the same pattern. Account one posts haikus, account two proverbs, account three rambling prose, and so forth."

"So these guys are talking to each other."

"Yes."

"Can you analyze these patterns in past communications?"

"Past communications? Like *all* past communications?"

"I just want to know if these guys have been talking for a while. Maybe we can decipher the code."

"I'll send it to headquarters to work on it."

"Good work."

He started to leave, but before he left, Jess caught his arm and said, "Jake, you're right. The next attack will come soon. Look at this."

She showed him a post that read, "Coming soon! A spectacular explosion that will enliven the spirits of all who bear witness! Not for the faint of heart, though! If you're not careful, you might get hurt too!"

Jake gave Jess a sober look. "Find this guy," he said. "We need to know who he is and what he's planning."

"On it."

Jake read the message again. Its jocular tone incensed him.

You think killing people is funny, asshole? All right. Keep it up. We'll see if you laugh when I meet you.

CHAPTER FOUR

Jake and Jess spent the rest of the day trying to trace the IP addresses used to create the posts Jess flagged as suspicious. Jess had extensive knowledge of technology, but the IP addresses were protected by very good VPNs which distributed their network across computers around the world, and by the end of the day, they were no closer to identifying their terrorists.

"I'm gonna call it," Jess finally said after actually finishing a cup of coffee—this one something called a Mayan Mocha—whatever that was. "I have a contact at the NSA. I'll send him the footage and the social media posts and see if he can find something for me."

"How do you have a contact at the NSA?"

She lifted her eyebrow knowingly. "Do you really want to know?"

Jake decided he didn't. With the investigation gaining no traction and nothing to do but wait until they had a lead, he decided to pay a visit to his old friend, Max.

Maxwell Harrison was a former Master Gunnery Sergeant and chief of sniper instruction at the School of Infantry (West) at Camp Pendleton, California. Before that, he was the most decorated sniper in Marine Corps history with over two hundred confirmed kills. He served as a sniper from 1988 to 2007 and an instructor after that until 2022. He had taught Jake how to be a sniper when Jake attended the course in 2008. The two men had remained good friends ever since.

These days, Max ran his own bar in the D.C. suburb of Falls Church, Virginia. The bar, rather cheekily named The Sniper's Den, was themed more like a hunting lodge than a military barracks. Considering the similarities between a sniper's duties and a big game hunter's typical behavior, Jake thought the décor appropriate.

As he navigated the ever-present traffic of the Beltway, Jake ruminated on the case. He very rarely felt in over his head in life, but he felt that way now. He understood Art's thought process. He was concerned for the President's safety and justifiably concerned that the other agencies cared more for the prestige that solving the case would offer, but just because Jake had better motivations didn't mean he was more qualified.

Then again, he had only felt this way once the case was officially his. Before Art gave him official status, he intended to commandeer the direction of the case regardless of the official decision.

So what was he really afraid of?

That was what he hoped Max could tell him. The man had become something of a father figure to Jake. He still talked to his parents, but their relationship had been strained ever since Jake joined the Corps. His parents pushed hard for him to go to school and get his degree in a professional field, but Jake had his heart set on the Marine Corps since he saw his hometown's Veterans Day Parade when he was twelve years old.

Recalling the patriotic parade reminded him of his thoughts just prior to the assault at the Lincoln Memorial. He frowned and let the memory drift through his mind.

Trident had chosen their target well. Terrorist militias like Trident clearly couldn't hope to win anything resembling a direct conflict with a government, especially not the United States government. The one thing they could do was exactly what their name suggested—terrorize. It was even possible that Trident didn't intend to kill the President. Forcing him to flee from a scene where six people had been killed would be enough to cause an uproar and give Trident a chance to foment dissatisfaction with the government.

His frown deepened as he recalled the President's insistence that he return to the White House as soon as possible. He was adamant that he show that the terrorist attack didn't affect him, and Jake was beginning to understand why.

But that didn't mean Jake was wrong. The President was still in danger. Jake's job was to ensure that he was safe.

Dammit, Trident had put them in an unwinnable position. Show strength, and the President risked assassination. Play it safe, and he appeared spineless.

Whoever was behind this attack was very intelligent and that made them very dangerous.

He parked in front of the Sniper's Den and saw that there were only a few cars in the lot. He had beaten the late-night rush. That would give him a few minutes alone with Max.

He walked inside to find the older man leaning over the counter chatting up a girl who looked about Jess's age. That made her ten years younger than Jake and thirty years younger than Max.

Max never flirted seriously. He used his charm and gravitas to make his clients feel special, but Jake had never known Max to ever act on the attraction that nearly all women seemed to feel for him.

This woman clearly enjoyed the attention, though. She flashed Jake an irritated look when Max excused himself and left to greet his old friend. Jake smiles slightly, and as he embraced Max, he whispered, "Should I come back? I think this one really likes you."

"They all really like me," Max whispered back, "but my life, my love, my lady is the Corps."

"And yet here you are serving cocktails and beer nuts."

"And here you are coming to whine to me about what a pompous ass Bryan is now that he's President."

"Bryan's always been an ass," Jake said, "but he's an honest ass, so we forgive him for it."

The three men had been acquaintances from back when Bryan Jackson was a Congressman. Jake was finishing the last three weeks of his service at Pendleton doing odd jobs the officers and Senior NCOs didn't want to deal with—such as escorting visiting Congressmen. Max had joined them at Bryan's request since he was somewhat of a celebrity in the Corps. Bryan's grandfather had fought at Iwo Jima, and while Bryan had elected to pursue politics rather than military service, he retained a deep love for the Corps that persisted into his administration.

The three men had struck an unlikely friendship, and when Jake applied to the Secret Service, Bryan used his connections to ensure that Jake was assigned to the President's security detail without having to slog his way up the Secret Service Ladder.

Jake wondered if Bryan questioned that choice now.

Max brought Jake a shot of whiskey, and before he drank it, he said, "This is American whiskey, right? Not that Scotch bullshit you gave me last time."

Max shook his head. "You know, you're the kind of kid who would go to a steakhouse and ask for mac and cheese. But yes, it's good old-fashioned Tennessee whiskey, not the thirty-year Macallan that I'm apparently going to have to drink myself since no one here seems to want it. You know even the senators turned it down?"

"That's because they know good whiskey," Jake said, sipping his liquor.

"I assure you they do not," Max said, "but they tip well."

"Really?"

Max grinned. "Well, I make sure to tell them about the time I took out Akram in the whorehouse."

Jake laughed, narrowly avoiding spitting his whiskey on Max. "I remember that. That was a good day."

"Well, I don't know how good a day it is when it ends in killing a man, but I'll take it."

"It's a good day when the man you kill is responsible for the deaths of hundreds of innocents."

"Thousands. And point taken. Anyway, the military is back in vogue now, so no politician who wants to keep his job is going to let it be known that he stiffed a decorated Marine Corps veteran."

"Well, I'm glad they're scared of you. It's good for politicians to be afraid."

"But not always, right?"

Jake met Max's eyes and saw a shrewd look. The older man had guessed at the real reason for Jake's visit. Jake finished his whiskey and said, "If you agree to drink some of it with me, I'll go ahead and try a shot of that Scotch crap."

"if you drink it and still consider it crap, I might have to reconsider our friendship," Max replied, "but with that caveat in mind, I will join you."

The two men took a table near the back of the bar. Other than the woman, who probably only hung around in case Max decided to talk to her again, there were two other women and a man who didn't realize that said women were only tolerating his clumsy jokes so he would keep buying them drinks.

Another girl came out from behind the bar and took over Max's duties, smiling at the woman at the counter and offering her a drink.

"My niece," Max said, "so don't get any ideas."

"Relax," Jake said, "I'm not stupid."

"We'll agree to disagree on that. So what's going on?"

Jake sighed. "Art wants me to lead the investigation into the assassination attempt."

"And that's a bad thing?"

Jake shrugged. "I'm not a cop, Max. I'm supposed to keep the President safe, not investigate crimes."

"Finding and apprehending the people responsible for endangering the President seems like a good way to keep him safe."

"Yes, but I'm not the guy who finds them, I'm the guy who takes them out. If Art wanted the FBI to lead the investigation but send me to pull the trigger when we find them, I'd be all for it. But this casework stuff?" He shook his head, "there's a reason I didn't become an officer."

Max laughed loudly at that. "Jake, if you honestly think the officers did anything that involved using their minds, then you didn't pay attention. The officers' job was to tell their NCOs what needed to be done, then stay the hell out of the way while we did it."

"You know what I mean, Max."

Max lifted an eyebrow. "Wow. You're really worried about this."

Jake shrugged. "There's a lot at stake here, Max."

Max nodded. "Yeah, I know. Do you want the kind, fatherly advice or the Master Gunny advice?"

"Does the Master Gunny advice go something like, 'Suck it the fuck up and stop being a bitch?'"

"Something like that. It also goes, 'Focus on the objective and don't pay attention to the noise. That's your spotter's job.'"

Jake nodded. "I do have a pretty good spotter."

"You do. She's also a pretty spotter. You sure you're not interested?"

"Nope. All yours."

Max rolled his eyes. "I walked into that. I don't mean for me, I mean for you."

Jake chuckled. "Nah, she's a friend. Nothing more."

"That's too bad. You could use good female company."

Jake didn't want the conversation to drift toward his personal life, so he sipped his whiskey instead. He grimaced and said, "Jesus. What the hell do they make this with? Bathwater?"

Max sighed and hung his head. "You do your best, you know? But sometimes, they're just too stupid to learn."

Jake rolled his eyes. "Whatever. You enjoy your bathwater. I'll drink American whiskey."

His phone buzzed, and when he saw Jess's number, his smile vanished. He answered, and Jess said, "Jake, my NSA contact called me back. They traced one of the social media accounts back to a known member of Trident. I compared his picture with the four men we saw in the video from the Lincoln Memorial. He's one of the assassins."

"I'm on my way."

He hung up and stood. He reached for his wallet, and Max said, "If your hand comes out of that pocket with a wallet in its grasp, I'm going to rip it off of your wrist and slap you silly with it."

Jake lifted his hand—sans wallet—and said, "Normally I'd argue with you, but I have a big lead I have to follow up on."

"Follow up on it then. What the hell are you doing here?"

Jake chuckled. "I'll see you later, Max. Thank you."

"You're welcome. Head up and teeth bared, Marine. Those assholes are dead already. You're just enjoying the hunt. Remember that."

"I'll do my best."

He left the bar and headed back to D.C. feeling a little better about things. He still wasn't sure he was the best person for this job, but either way, the President would be kept safe.

He would bet his life on that.

CHAPTER FIVE

Jake had thought that investigating the case would be his least favorite part of this job.

This was worse.

He swerved hard to avoid hitting a panel truck that had screeched to a halt to avoid t-boning the suspect's motorcycle. His rear wheel spun out, and he slid his bike a good ten yards before he was able to right it. When he resumed his pursuit, the suspect was nearly two hundred yards ahead.

"Dammit," he swore. "Jess, I'm going to lose him. Do you have eyes?"

"As long as he stays in the city proper, I do. If he heads to the suburbs, I might be out of luck."

"Well, let's cross our finger."

Jake revved his motor and the Harly launched forward. It was a good bike, powerful, stable and fast, but it lacked the agility of the sports bike the suspect rode. When the Trident member turned and saw Jake gaining, he veered down a side street almost effortlessly while Jake was forced to brake hard and turn much more carefully.

The NSA had traced one of the suspicious posts to a man named Gunnar Jefferson. Jake had gone to question Gunnar only to have the man speed away on his sports bike as Jake was walking to the door.

And now Jake was riding his motorcycle on a high-speed chase through one of the most congested traffic spots in the country. As he weaved through cars and skidded down alleys, he gritted his teeth and said a silent prayer that he wouldn't hit anyone while he chased Gunnar.

Gunnar was thirty-two years old, and according to the information Jess could find, he was quite the character. Four arrests for assault, one aggravated, three for armed robbery, two burglary and more petty theft convictions than Jake had bothered to count.

That was fairly typical for men involved in these fringe groups. Organizations like Trident appealed to men who felt rejected or cheated or hopeless. They gave these men a target to focus on other than themselves, something they could blame for the hardship in their lives without having to take responsibility for their own actions.

But Gunnar's behavior—and all of Trident's—had escalated far beyond rabblerousing. They had attempted to assassinate the President of the United States and killed six people in the process, and Jake would be damned if he lost Gunnar now.

"He's trying to head for Maryland," Jess said, "Cut him off."

Jake turned right, losing sight of Gunnar as he tried to position his bike ahead of the fleeing criminal. "Talk to me, Jess."

"He's to your left. He's slowing down. He thinks he's lost you."

"Well, he's got another thing coming."

Jake gunned the motor, carefully choosing lines that would require the least amount of correction. When he reached a wide intersection, he turned left, continuing to accelerate through the turn. He looked at his speedometer and promptly wished that he hadn't.

When he turned right in front of Gunnar, though, the speed and the risk that came with it was worth it. The man's eyes widened, and for a split second, Jake was sure he had him. He gunned his motor and reached for Gunnar.

Then Gunnar slid his bike in a circle, diving under Jake's hand and continuing the opposite way Jake was riding. Jake swore and spun his own bike around, but the heavy cruiser bike took a moment to regain speed, and when it did, Gunnar was once more over a hundred yards ahead of Jake.

Gunnar knew he was nimbler and took advantage of this, veering down alleys and into parks and sidewalks where Jake had to struggle to remain upright, let alone follow.

But still, Jake kept up. This man was one of the assassins that had threatened the President, and Jake would catch him regardless of the advantage the man held in maneuverability.

That task proved easier said than done. Twice more, Jake nearly reached Gunnar, and twice more, the Trident member pulled off some stunt-worthy maneuver to avoid Jake.

Jake wished he could just post up on a rooftop somewhere and shoot the man. It didn't matter how nimble he was if Jake had his rifle with him. He had hit moving targets before. It was no problem for him.

The problem was that while nearly any measure could be taken to ensure the President's safety, it would take a lot more than the current circumstances for Jake to get away with shooting Gunnar.

“He’s got to be running out of fuel, right?” Jake said as the chase neared the thirty-minute mark. “How much gas do those crotch rockets carry?”

“That model is a turbocharged low-displacement twin,” Jess informed him. “It uses far less fuel than your bike does. You have twenty more miles of road range than he does, but in a high-speed chase like this, there’s really no way to tell who will run out of gas first.”

“Can we get Washington PD to put a spike strip down or something?”

“I asked, but they said you two are driving too recklessly. They want you to cease pursuit and let them put an APB out.”

“Tell them to put the APB out anyway. And tell them that if they don’t want me to drive recklessly, they need to get their shit together and stop this guy.”

Gunnar veered off of the crowded road onto a farm-to-market road that led into the Virginia countryside. Jake realized they had made it to the edge of Washington. Traffic was thinner here, and finally, Jake had the advantage.

He gunned his throttle, and the burly Harley slowly but surely closed the distance on the little sports bike. Gunnar looked wildly around for an option, but there was nothing on either side of him but fields and rolling hillsides. Neither of their bikes was built for off-pavement, but the Harley’s greater weight, tire size and wheelbase accompanied with its torquier engine would give it an even greater advantage if Gunnar did decide to take the chase that way.

Of course, he didn’t. What he did instead was leap off his bike and kick it down suddenly. Jake swore and tried to avoid the impact, but his rear tire caught the front tire of Gunnar’s fallen bike. The shearing force of the wheel spinning perpendicular to his own caused him to fishtail wildly.

He struggled with the out-of-control Harley, twisting the handlebars and pumping the throttle to try to get the bike headed in the right direction, or any direction, really.

If he were riding a little sports bike like the one Gunnar abandoned, he probably would have wiped out too, but the Harley had a fat rear tire and a low center of gravity, and though he seesawed sickeningly several times before he finally righted, he kept from crashing or falling off the side of the road.

By the time he did gain control, though, Gunnar was gone. His bike must have somehow survived the crash because it was gone too. It was clear that he had managed to get back on and ride away while Jake was spinning out of control.

Frustration bubbled up in Jake and quickly turned into rage. He had lost him. He had actually lost him. He had a chance to apprehend one of the men responsible for attacking the President, and he had fucking lost him.

"Goddammit!" he shouted. "Dammit."

He pulled his bike to a stop and got off to allow his heart rate to calm down. He shook his head and tapped his earpiece. "Jess, I lost him. He spun me out and somehow managed to save his own bike and ride off."

"Are you all right?" she asked, concerned.

"Yeah, I'm fine. I didn't wipe all the way out, I just lost control for a moment. That's all it took though. Dammit!"

"Take a breath, Jake," Jess said with uncharacteristic sternness. "We know he's one of the men we're looking for now. That's good information. We can use that. Relax, and come on back to headquarters. We'll figure this out."

As far as pep talks went, this one was less than helpful, but that wasn't Jess's fault. There wasn't much at all that would help Jake overcome his frustration. He sighed and said, "All right. I'm on my way."

He tapped his earpiece again and prepared to leave, but as soon as he started his bike, he saw something that caught his eye.

He shut his engine off and approached the object. It gleamed dully in the bright sunlight, and when Jake reached it, he recognized the drab green casing of an AN/PRC-117G portable radio.

He felt a touch of satisfaction at that and tapped his earpiece. "Hey, Jess. Gunnar dropped his radio. I'm bringing it to the lab for analysis."

"See? It wasn't a complete waste of time."

He chuckled and said drily. "Gee, thanks."

"Oh, quit grousing. I know you Marine Corps types don't like to lose, but it's only the first quarter for God's sake. There's plenty of time to catch up."

"I could spend all day telling you why that's the worst possible thing you could say to me."

"And I could counter it all by telling you to suck it up and get your ass back on reservation for a debriefing or you're on latrine duty for the rest of deployment."

Jake laughed out loud at that, and he was pleased to see that much of his anger had dissipated after the conversation. "All right. I'm on my way."

He had to take a circuitous route to headquarters, taking the Beltway all the way to the Maryland side and coming in the opposite way. Jess had told him that local cops were looking for him, although they didn't know it was him, of course.

It probably wouldn't make a difference if they did. Local cops were particularly sore about traffic violations.

He reached headquarters just before lunchtime. Jess was waiting for him in the lobby, arms crossed.

"Uh oh," he said, "Am I in trouble?"

Jess glared at him, and he lifted an eyebrow. "Oh. I really *am* in trouble."

"Jake Mercer, you are not Rambo."

Jake sighed. "Rambo was a Green Beret. That's U.S. Army, not Marines."

"Exactly."

"I don't think you're making the point you think you're making, Jess."

"My point is you need to be careful! Remember what I said, this is the first quarter. We have time to win the game, but if our star running back blows out his knee, we have a lot smaller of a chance. Stop acting like a damned cowboy."

Jake frowned. "What was I supposed to do? Not try?"

"You're supposed to acknowledge when a tactical retreat is the correct choice under the circumstances and preserve the integrity of your fighting units for future operations."

That was impressively close to real Marine lingo for a civilian, but Jake wasn't going to let Jess know that. "A tactical what? A reach-reet? What's that?"

She rolled her eyes and turned away, stalking toward the elevator. Jake lifted the radio and called after her. "Aren't you forgetting something?"

"I'm not. Bring it with you."

Jake tucked the radio back into his bag and followed Jess. He was still pissed about losing Gunnar, but for all his teasing, Jess was right. They had gained a valuable piece of evidence in that radio. They may not have won the battle yet, but they hadn't lost either.

CHAPTER SIX

The time had come to bring the President and his family home. Three days, Bryan argued, was more than enough time to satisfy the need for caution. Trident had gone quiet, and no sign of attack had arisen since the Lincoln Memorial assault. Any further hiding would show him and the nation to be spineless, and he wouldn't stand for that.

Jake grudgingly had to admit that he was right. Not about the lack of risk. Jess had been working nonstop to decode the radio Jake found, even reaching out to contacts in other agencies, but the radio was protected by a sophisticated firewall that proved incredibly resilient. It could be a while before they decoded it and then it might be too late.

But they could no longer justify keeping the President in hiding. People wanted to see that their leader was stronger than the people who had threatened his life. They wanted to see him at the front of the fight to bring those killers to justice, not locked in a hidden bunker being waited on hand and foot.

So, he sat in his small office in Outpost Alpha and worked on mapping the President's route back to the White House.

Actually, the mapping part was easy. They would simply lead the President through the tunnels. What was difficult was trying to figure out a way to protect the areas vulnerable to attack. It would be suicide for Trident to try to enter the tunnels and assassinate the President, but it would be very easy for them to place bombs at certain points to collapse the tunnels. In some places, less than ten feet separated the tunnel roof from the street. A decently sized wad of C4 would penetrate that easily.

"Knock-knock," a soft voice called.

Jake felt a rush of heat followed instantly by a rush of cold. When he lifted his eyes to the shimmering blue spheres of Sheila Jackson, he settled into a comfortable warmth.

Sheila smiled, a touch hesitantly, and asked, "May I come in?"

"Of course, ma'am," Jake said formally—too formally.

Sheila smiled again, and her eyes made it clear that she saw right through Jake's façade. She walked toward him, and Jake was convinced she made her hips sway that way on purpose.

He was easily able to stifle any attraction he might feel toward Jess in the interest of maintaining a professional distance, but with Sheila, it was impossible. He thought of Max's probing into his love life the night before, and a frown played at his lips. If Max knew where Jake's interests truly lay, he would immediately warn Jake to soak his head in ice water until his brain started working again.

The problem was that there was no way for his brain to work right around Sheila. She sat across from him, and frowning was impossible.

"How's it going?" she asked.

"Well, ma'am," he said.

"Please don't call me ma'am," Sheila asked.

It was spoken softly and with a smile, but it wasn't a request. Jake swallowed and said, "Miss Jackson—"

"Sheila," she insisted.

Dammit, Sheila, I can't.

"It's going well," he said, avoiding the use of her name. "We've determined the identity of one of your father's attackers, and we've recovered a key piece of evidence that will provide a wealth of information our investigative team can use."

"The radio?"

Jake cursed inwardly and wondered if it would make any difference if he asked Bryan to stop spying on the Secret Service and just allow them to do their jobs. Probably not, and anyway, he wasn't close enough to the man that it was advisable for him to question his judgment.

Well, there was no point in playing coy. "Yes."

"Have you been able to read it yet?"

"Well, it doesn't record information, it only transmits it."

"There's not a record of the radio channel used?"

"We're looking into that now."

The NSA frequently monitored ham radio channels since many of these low-level terrorist militias used amateur radio to communicate to their followers. Of course, Trident wasn't low-level anymore. They had leapfrogged all the way to the major leagues.

"So no."

She said it gently, but her words still cut Jake like a knife. "No. Nothing yet. NSA's checking records, but everyone speaks in code on the radio. It's hard to know what's suspicious and what's a couple of stupid teenagers playing spy."

She nodded and looked away. She bit her lip, and Jake had to stifle an urge to do something that would almost certainly get him fired regardless of how close he was to the President. Sheila didn't help when she looked at him, eyes shining with concern, and asked, "Are you all right, Jake? Really? Jess told me you nearly killed yourself on the road the other day."

So that's who Sheila talked to. Jake stifled the urge to roll his eyes. Jess knew about his attraction to Sheila because Jess was really his mother packaged in a younger body. And now she was using the girl he liked to try to pressure him into being more careful.

In the back of his mind, Jake realized how crazy he sounded, but with Sheila barely three feet away, his head refused to work the way it should. He decided to deal with his convoluted fantasy later and only said, "Jess was… mistaken. I pursued a suspect past the Beltway, and unfortunately collided with his motorcycle. I was able to maintain an upright position on the motorcycle, but while I recovered, the suspect was able to escape. I was angry, but not hurt."

Sheila nodded, but she didn't seem relieved. He shifted in his chair and said, "I'm fine, Sheila."

She nodded again. "Just please remember that I need you. To keep my father safe."

He smiled. "Of course."

Sheila stood and crossed her arms, pacing back and forth in front of him. God, it was like every move she made was designed to enchant him! She had a natural grace that reminded Jake of royalty. Combined with her kind heart and the sort of beauty that only came along once in a thousand generations, she was the picture of every dream of love Jake had ever had.

"I'm worried about my father," she said finally. "I understand that he needs to be brave, and he wants to show the world that we won't give in to terrorist demands, but I hate knowing that people want to kill him just because of his job.

"That's the worst part."

She came to a stop and turned to him. Her eyes blazed, and her cheeks flushed with color. Jake felt a stab of guilt at the way he reacted to that flush, but he couldn't help himself. She was just as beautiful angry as she was at all other times.

"They don't even care about his politics. It doesn't matter what he stands for or what he believes in. It doesn't even matter if it's him standing up there or anyone else with the same title. They just hate authority, and because they hate authority, they want to kill whoever wields it, whether they're good or not."

"I won't let that happen, Sheila."

She continued to rant as though she didn't hear what he said. Jake imagined she had bottled these feelings up for a while, and once she got started releasing them, she couldn't stop. "It's just so stupid! They're so stupid! For all they care to find out, my father might actually be helping them! So why do they want to kill him? And those people…"

The color faded from her cheeks, her defiant expression wavered, and her lower lip began to tremble.

Jake acted without thinking. He was on his feet with his arms around her before his mind registered what he was doing, and by then, it was too late to stop. He pulled her close, and she melted into his arms, bursting into tears.

She wrapped her arms around his shoulders and buried her face in his neck, and she felt so, so good. Her body was warm and yielding in his grasp, and her breath was hot against his throat as she wept. He wanted to protect her, to shield her from everything in this world that would try to hurt her. He wanted to carry her somewhere far away where she wouldn't have to worry about assassins attacking her family.

He wanted to hold her and never let her go.

"I just hate that they killed those poor people. They were so excited to see Dad! They just wanted to have fun and tell their families all about their trip to the capital. I just… how do you do that? How do you kill innocent people like that?"

How the hell do you make an innocent civilian carry a bomb?

Jake had killed forty-six men this far in his career as a sniper. In all forty-six cases, his finger had never wavered on the trigger.

But it wavered now. The woman standing in the middle of the street with a vest filled with dynamite clearly didn't want to be there. She shook and wept as soldiers in front of her shouted at her to stop while insurgents behind shouted for her to walk forward.

How the hell do you recruit civilians? How do you look at an innocent woman and tell her to carry a vest?

"Cowards," he growled under his breath. "They're all cowards."

"Yes, they are, Jake, and we'll get them for this, but right now, you need to keep your aim on the target."

His spotter, Staff Sergeant Ben Hendricks, betrayed his own emotion in his thin whisper, but Jake knew that he would do whatever needed to be done, no matter how painful.

Jake wasn't sure he could.

"That's not a target, Ben, that's a civilian. She's fucking innocent!"

"I know, Jake. I know."

Jake swore under his breath and prayed silently.

Please turn around. Please just turn around.

The woman did turn around, and Jake released a breath. Thank God.

A gunshot rang out, and before Jake could process what he was seeing—

"Thank you."

Jake blinked and realized that Sheila had stopped crying and was now waiting for him to release her so she could stand. He straightened quickly and hoped the flush in his cheeks wasn't visible.

The flush in Sheila's cheeks was clearly visible, and Jake couldn't be sure that the look in her eyes was only his imagination. He cleared his throat and took an extra step back.

"I'll do everything in my power to ensure your father's safety, Sheila. And yours."

Sheila smiled, a little sadly. "I know you will. Thank you, Jake."

He cleared his throat. "I'm going to review last-minute checks with my team, then we'll start heading for the White House. Do you need anything from me before I go?"

Sheila gave him another wistful smile. "No. You've done enough."

He was sure her words were innocent, but they stung, nonetheless. He managed a smile, then turned and left before he found another way to make a fool out of himself.

He was keenly aware of Sheila's eyes on his back as he left the room.

His earpiece buzzed, and Jess said, "All right, Jake o'lantern. You're looking solid above ground. Nothing suspicious to report except a couple of bums caught peeing against a wall."

"Roger that. Detail Sigma is prepared to transport the package."

"Really? Not even a groan? I put a lot of work into Jake lantern."

Jake chuckled softly. "It was a good one."

"Are you okay? You sound depressed."

"I'm fine. I'll talk to you soon."

He hung up, took a deep breath and squared his shoulders. His heartbreak could wait.

He had work to do.

CHAPTER SEVEN

Jake led the team through the tunnel to the White House. The President, his wife, Carrie, and Sheila stood in the middle of a dozen agents armed with assault rifles and riot gear.

Jake could feel sweat trickling into his eyes. He would have to purchase a sweat band so this didn't happen again. He kicked himself for not thinking about that earlier. As a Marine Corps sniper, he had always worn a sweat band. A sniper's vision was critical, and anything that could compromise it—including sweat—had to be addressed proactively. If Trident found them in here while Jake was blinking sweat away, then his lack of preparation could mean the death of the President and his family.

Dammit, he wanted this solved. He wanted the perpetrators behind bars. He wanted the President safe, and he wanted Sheila safe, and he wanted those killers put somewhere they could never get out.

Every step felt like a thousand years to Jake. When they finally reached the White House, he was almost surprised that nothing had happened. He looked back at the faces of his agents and saw similar surprise on their faces. After learning of the threat of another attack, Jake had been all but certain that attack would take place now.

He was reminded of battles during his service with the Corps. At times, the silence could be even worse than combat. At least in combat, you knew where the enemy was and what he was doing. When nothing was happening, you didn't know if the enemy was ahead of you, behind you, or all around you.

The team split off as planned. Four agents led Carrie and Sheila away. Sheila cast a quick glance Jake's way but said nothing as she followed her mother to the family's living quarters. The remaining agents, including Jake, followed the President to the Oval Office.

Bryan smiled at Jake when they reached the office safely. "See? Nothing to worry about."

Jake nodded but didn't say anything in reply. He stayed until the President was settled into the office, then left four agents outside the door and headed back to headquarters.

The President hadn't been attacked yet, but an attack was coming. If they wanted to stop it, they needed the information on the radio.

He headed to Jess's office and found her still poring over the radio. "How much longer?" he asked.

Jess looked at her screen. "Too soon to tell," she replied.

The radio sat on a metal tray Jess assured him was sterile. He wasn't certain why being sterile mattered much, but Jess was the tech expert, not him. Jake wasn't new to technology, but he had never bothered to glean more than a surface knowledge of it. He didn't even know this radio had a means to store data until Jess looked at it and told him it did.

In contrast, there was a graceful, almost fluid ease with which Jess approached technology. Her approach inspired confidence on one level. On another level, it just highlighted for Jake how out of touch he felt.

"What are we waiting for?" he asked.

"We're waiting for confirmation that this isn't going to explode," Jess said brightly, "sending shrapnel flying outward like death ducks in *V* formation."

"Death ducks? Did I really just hear that?"

She shrugged. "I'm binging an anime when I'm not busy protecting the leader of the free world."

"An anime with death ducks?"

"Yep! Cute ones too," she replied. "All right. There's no danger in this communicator, at least not any explosive danger."

"What about tracking?"

"No tracking devices either."

"Outstanding. So we should be good to open it up, right?"

"Open it up? You mean crack the firewall and extract the data?"

"Yeah. There's not a memory card or something?"

Jess stared at him incredulously. "God, I forget how old you are sometimes."

"Screw you."

"I'm afraid I'd break you if we tried."

He rolled his eyes and said, "Okay, are we good to extract the data by whatever means is appropriate to this new-fangled contraption that the kids dreamed up as an affront to God and nature?"

She laughed, and while it was an agreeable sound, Jake couldn't help but compare it to the angelic music of Sheila's voice. He rubbed his eyes. God, he was tired.

"Okay, old man. Why don't you go get us some coffee and donuts, and I'll take a peek at the firewall and see what we're looking at. Be careful not to trip on the way to the cafeteria."

"You must be tired too. Your humor's slipping."

"I'm exhausted. That's why I'm sending you for coffee."

"Why don't *you* get the coffee."

"Sure. Can you check the firewall for kill switches and erasers? It's not likely there's any kind of data mining or transmission capability that could penetrate the room's EM-hardening, but you might as well check that too. Oh, and if you do get to the code, make sure the decrypting software you run is set to the correct programming language so you don't corrupt the data."

"I'll go get the coffee."

"Cream and sugar, please!"

The cafeteria was nearly empty. The Secret Service operated around the clock, but the headquarters building followed a more or less typical nine-to-five schedule. Agents flitted in and out before or after their shifts, and on rare occasions during, but once the President and his family were safely asleep under multiple layers of protection, the agency went as close to dormant as it ever did.

It wasn't quite as dead here as it normally would be. The Lincoln Memorial attack was still the hot topic of conversation, and everyone walked on eggshells waiting for a lead on the perpetrators or the bad news of another attack. Still, Jake counted only a dozen other agents in a room that could sit over three hundred.

He made coffee for the two of them and grabbed a donut for Jess and a breakfast burrito for himself. After debating a moment, he grabbed a burrito for Jess as well. Jess had the terrible habit of needing to try everything he ate, and it was a pet peeve of his that she seemed to have no trouble taking a bite of his food without asking.

He returned to Jess's lab and said, "I got you a burrito too. You don't have to eat it, but if you get the urge to eat mine, just eat yours instead."

Jess leaned back from her workstation. She had her arms crossed, and she was biting her lip. That meant she was nervous.

"What is it?" he asked.

She shook her head. "The encryption algorithm they're using is incredibly sophisticated."

"On a standard issue radio?"

"This radio isn't standard issue," she said. "Do you know what a sleeper car is?"

"Yes. It's a car that looks slow but it's actually fast."

"Well, that's what this is. It looks like a radio, but it's actually a portable computer. If it wanted to be, it could be the best smartphone the world has ever seen. Instead, it's the world's most overpowered satellite phone."

"I'm not sure what the difference is between a satellite phone and a smartphone."

"I'll tell you later. My point now is that it's going to take a long time to get anything useful off of this."

"Really? It's that tough?"

"It's that tough. I could tell you exactly why, but you wouldn't understand the tech lingo. The best analogy I can give is that it's like trying to untie a knot, but every time you untie it, you just reach another knot."

"Can you get in?"

"Yeah, I can get in," she said, "It's just going to take a while."

"How long is a while?"

"Long enough that I need you to hand me my coffee so I can put up with your nagging while I work."

He handed her the coffee and asked, "Can I help?"

"Yes. I'm going to give you some things to look up in the NSA database."

"You mean to ask your contact to look up."

"No, he gave me his login information."

Jake stared at her, and she said, "You don't want to know."

"Jesus Christ, did you say you were going to marry this guy?"

She chuckled. "Believe me, marriage isn't what he wants. And anyway, he got his boss's permission to let me access the database. We *are* trying to keep the President from being killed after all."

"Well, good for you, and good for him too, it sounds."

She fixed a sultry smile on him and said, "*Very* good."

They worked through the night. From time to time, Jess gave Jake tasks, mostly serial numbers for some of the technology used in the radio. A lot of the technology was bleeding-edge military tech earmarked for special operators. Some of it was experimental, and the encryption software was nowhere to be found on the NSA's database. That meant it was either the most classified of classified items or it was proprietary.

One thing was sure, though. Trident had access to incredibly sophisticated technology.

“They would have to be incredibly well-funded to have access to this,” Jake opined. “Foreign help?”

“It’s possible. Or it’s possible that they have friends in high places. Have you considered that one of the President’s political rivals could be behind the assassination.”

“It’s an angle I’ve considered,” Jake said, “but we haven’t found anything to connect to any member of Congress, and I can’t see even the most backwards of lawmakers risking their own lives working with a group as volatile and dangerous as Trident.”

“Well, whoever’s funding them has access to the big bucks.”

“Have you learned anything at all?”

“So far, I’ve just confirmed the identities of the four men in the video. We know about Gunnar Jefferson. We know about Tanner Wilson—that’s the one you killed. The other three are LeShaun Mays, Isak Czeny and Walter Ford. I’ve sent the names to the FBI to get them started on the manhunt. All three men have PO boxes instead of residences as their registered addresses.”

“What about the one who got away?” Jake asked, “the one who wasn’t on the camera?”

“He’s still a ghost. It doesn’t look like he’s anywhere on these chats.”

“So you have the names of the individuals but no chat data yet?”

“Exactly. I can tell you that they coordinated the Lincoln Memorial attack very thoroughly. I can’t read what they said to each other, but there’s a linear curve of calls placed and received that ramps up twenty-four hours before the assassination attempt and peaks one hour before the van arrived at the National Mall. There’s two hours of silence, then another spike that lasts for two more hours before dropping off entirely.”

“A debriefing.”

“That’s my guess.”

He sighed. “This reminds me of when we were monitoring radio traffic to track down Ahsan Abdullah.”

“Who’s Ahsan Abdullah?”

“He *was* a terrorist leader hiding out in Tajikistan and planning an assault on the UN headquarters in New York. I was assigned with a Seal Team to take him out. We knew he was going to travel into Afghanistan, but we didn’t know when. The best we could do was monitor radio traffic. The team we were on didn’t have an interpreter because he was well-connected in Afghanistan, and we didn’t want to risk someone grabbing the interpreter and learning of the op, so we just looked for spikes in radio traffic. When we found one at a small village near the border, we knew that he was going to pass through. We waited for him there, and… well, we were successful."

"That's good to know. I'll have the NSA monitor these frequencies. If we see a spike, then… hold on."

Jake came instantly to high alert. "What is it?"

"I got something. It's a recent communication. It looks like one of the last messages Gunnar received before he lost this radio. I managed to decrypt a portion of the message."

"What does it say?"

"Moving parade."

"That's it?"

"Well, it's all I have."

Jake thought a moment. Then his eyes widened. "The Vice President is planning a public parade for Remembrance Day. It's traveling through the National Mall and up and down Pennsylvania Avenue. I'll bet anything that Trident is planning to attack again during that parade."

"Can we cancel it?" Jess asked.

"I can try," Jake said. He thought of the bullish, irascible Vice President Francis Sweeney and added, "but I won't succeed."

He and Jess shared a sober look. "Keep working on the data," Jake said. "Get whatever you can. I'll go talk to Art and see if we can beef up security for this event. The President has a closed-door meeting with the Defense Council that day, so at least he won't be there. I might be able to divert some more resources to protecting the VP."

"I'll keep working," she said. "Keep your head up, Jake. You've got this."

Jake didn't know he needed the encouragement until he heard it, but he smiled gratefully. "You too, Jess. I believe in you."

"Thank you, Daddy," Jess said with a grin.

He grimaced. "Eww. Don't call me that."

Jess's laughter followed him out of the room, but the brief lighthearted moment vanished as Jake made his way to Art's office.

Their enemy was no small-time alt-right fraternity. Trident was bankrolled by someone dangerous.

And they were on the hunt again.

CHAPTER EIGHT

Jake hated being away from the action.

He smiled grimly as he thought of the irony in that statement. Well, the apparent irony, anyway. Snipers were removed from the action in the sense that they weren't in the thick of most firefights. This was by necessity. A sniper needed to execute precise shots from long distances on high-value targets. They couldn't do this while also needing to worry for their own safety and adapt on a moment's notice to rapidly evolving circumstances.

In practice, the situation was rarely ideal. Snipers were often forced into close-range firefights, and especially in urban settings were constantly worried for their own safety. Experienced marksmen learned to balance the need to maintain eyes on their target with their need to be aware of a constantly shifting battlefield.

As a Secret Service agent assigned to the President's personal security detail, Jake was never away from action. Granted, up until the Lincoln Memorial bombing the week prior, the action was the constant vigilance against any action, but the fact remained that this was the first time Jake had felt helpless.

Helpless wasn't the right word either. Jake had oversight of the entire security operation involving hundreds of agents and officers from multiple agencies. He had cameras saturating the entire city and the authority to call for even more resources if he needed them.

So he wasn't helpless, he was just removed from the front lines.

He hated it.

To be fair, this entire parade was fucking stupid. The President had nearly been assassinated, and now the Vice President stubbornly insisted on a parade? It made no damned sense.

Trying to say that to the Vice President was about as pointless as trying to say that to the President. When Jake suggested that she reschedule or, better yet, cancel the parade altogether, she laughed in his face.

So now he was here trying to manage security for the sake of her bullshit vanity.

“You hanging in there, Jakey-Jake?” Jess asked.

“I liked Jake o’lantern better,” he quipped.

“Too late. I gave you a chance to adopt that nickname, and you ignored it. You’re Jakey-Jake now.”

“Lovely. Well, to answer your question, I feel like a spring about to explode.”

“I don’t think your analogy is quite clear,” Jess said, “but I get it. You want to be the grunt in the middle of the action, not the boss staring at computer screens.”

He sighed. “I understand why I’m here. My expertise is needed to oversee the entire situation from a birds’ eye view and react to evolving threats in the moment to ensure resources are directed appropriately.”

"Relax, Jake, I'm not Art. I was sympathizing with you, not testing your resolve."

“I was saying that for my benefit, not yours. It helps to remind myself I’m more useful up here than down there.”

“Well, keep that in mind, because her Royal Highness is on the move.”

Jake turned his attention to the center monitor. That monitor was programmed to always provide the closest aerial view of the Vice President.

Her Royal Highness was currently chafing over the need for the half-dozen heavily armed agents that surrounded her. She even more than the President wanted to flaunt her complete lack of fear, but she would have to satisfy herself with being allowed this parade and deal with the small army that existed to make sure she survived it.

The agents led her to the second of four identical limousines. When the motorcade arrived at The National Mall, she would stand and wave to the crowd, so they wouldn’t maintain secrecy as long as Jake would have liked, but the decoy vehicles gave Jake at least some measure of comfort that they could get her to the start of the parade unharmed.

He reached for one of five phones on the monitoring desk and called the special agent in charge of security along the parade route. “How are we looking, Gordon?”

“We’re looking all right,” Gordon said.

“All right? Why only all right?”

“There’s a lot of people here, Jake. If it becomes a firefight, there’s going to be collateral damage.”

Jake pressed his lips together. Collateral damage was exactly what he wanted to avoid. Collateral damage the last time had involved six eight-year-olds getting killed by flying shrapnel. Why the hell were so many people out here, anyway? Did they not remember that only a week ago there had been a terrorist attack in the National Mall?

"Just keep the streets clear. The faster we can get this parade done, the faster we can put this mess behind us."

"You got it, boss."

The motorcade began to drive. There were a dozen Capitol Police officers on motorcycles at the front of the motorcade. Behind them was an FBI SWAT van armored against anything smaller than a .50 caliber machine gun and sporting a smaller but still lethal 7.62mm machine gun on top. The four limos followed, flanked by two more motorcycle officers each. Behind the limos was another FBI van and another dozen motorcycles. The streets were lined with Washington PD officers with riot gear. Capitol Police helicopters orbited the parade, watching the ground for signs of any suspicious movement.

The Secret Service was everywhere in the National Mall. There were one hundred twenty uniformed officers on the ground under the supervision of ten Special Agents. Three Rapid Response Teams consisting of six highly trained officers each waited at the Washington Monument, the Martin Luther King, Jr. Memorial and the Thomas Jefferson Memorial.

This was as secure as Jake had ever seen the city.

So of course that meant the threat had to come from the one area they hadn't prepared for.

The motorcade reached the mall. Vice President Sweeney stood and smiled for the crowd. Jake monitored the various screens and checked in with each of his field team leads to ensure all was well.

Then Jess called, "Drone!"

Jake's blood froze. "Where?"

"Flying over the tidal basin off of Independence Avenue. It's moving fast."

Jake crossed to Jess's desk and looked at her screen. The drone was a civilian lookalike of the military's MQ-9 Reaper drone, scaled down to about one-fourth the size and painted in high-contrast white and orange to make it clear it was a civilian craft.

That did nothing to make the machine gun it carried any less lethal. The .50 caliber M2 it carried in a belly pod would rip through every vehicle in that motorcade like a hot knife through butter, and if it struck any people, they would be looking for pieces, not bodies.

Jake ran back to his workstation and pressed the emergency button that allowed him to communicate with all of his team leads at the same time.

“Code Red. We have a bogey inbound coming in hot over Independence Avenue. Moving northeast at seventy-five miles per hour. One heavy machine gun, unknown ammo capacity, but let’s assume it’s more than enough. Red, how soon can you intercept?”

Raul “Red” Ramos was in one of the three helicopter units managing the air component. “I can intercept, but I have no way of shooting it down. These are civilian choppers and unarmed. You know I’d fly into the bitch and kamikaze it if I could, but there’s too many people down there. If we come down on top of them, you’re looking at hundreds of casualties, easy.”

“No one’s kamikazeing anything,” Jake agreed. “What other options do we have?”

“National Guard, but they’re five minutes out. That drone is only two. I’m going to fly to intercept and hope its onboard radar tells it to avoid colliding with us.”

“Do that, but don’t get hit. You’re right about losing the chopper. Too many people at risk. Call the National Guard anyway. Maybe we’ll get lucky.”

“Will do.”

Jake turned his attention to the motorcade. The Vice President had already been pulled back into the vehicle, and the motorcade was proceeding along the preplanned evacuation route, but that route was planned assuming a ground assault. There was no protection from the air.

“Mike, can you get a shot?”

Mike was the leader of the four snipers positioned strategically throughout the mall. At the altitude at which the drone was flying, they would be the only people with a possible shot except for the FBI machine gunners, and Jake didn’t want to use them for the same reason Red didn’t want to fly his chopper into the drone.

“Negative, Jake. It’s moving too fast, and it’s moving against the wind.”

Jake cursed. “Any unusual activity on the ground at all?”

“Well, people are starting to panic now that they hear the drone coming, but nothing before that. Nothing that looks like the assholes last week.”

Dammit. Jake’s last bit of hope at getting through this without casualties was officially dashed. “Jill, can you take the drone out?”

Jill was the FBI lead. “We can try. The problem is that we’re going to be in range of that .50 before the drone is in range of our 7.62s. We have to hope it's on a predetermined flight path and that no one's controlling it."

"Split off from the motorcade and see if you can force it to divert away. We can at least get the VP out of here."

Jake's stomach roiled at having to order people possibly to their death, but this was combat. The VP was the high-value asset, and as brutal as it was to accept, everyone else was expendable.

He watched as the FBI vans deviated from the motorcade. Their path would take them behind the path of the drone, but as Jake monitored their trajectories, he could see that there would be a good ten seconds where the drone was in range of the vans but not close enough to the VPs vehicle.

"Come on," he whispered under his breath. "Come on."

The drone crept steadily closer to the FBI trap. Just when Jake thought they might have a shot, it's front camera swiveled toward the FBI vans. Then it's gun swiveled.

Shit. "Abort, Jill! Abort, abort, a—"

Too late. The front van had time to back up a few feet before a volley of thirteen-ounce shells ripped it open like a soda can. The next van got a volley of its own rounds off, but the drone veered sharply left, all the while maintaining its aim on the FBI van. The van burst into flames, and the drone corrected and resumed its pursuit of the Vice President.

Then the Capitol Police helicopters flew in front of it. "Come get some!" Ramos shouted through the radio.

The drone declined to get some. Instead, it dropped to just fifteen feet above ground level and weaved in between buildings lower than the helicopters could fly.

But that was close enough that the agents on the ground could shoot it.

"Fire!" Jake shouted. "Give it everything you've got!"

The screens lit up with the tiny flashes of light from the agents firing on the drone. The big .50 swiveled around, and Jake said, "Retreat! Get out of the way!"

Before the drone could fire, however, the cloud of nine-millimeter and 5.56 rounds finally took its toll. Its weapon kept swivelling around without aiming at anything. The drone dipped lazily to the left, and Jake saw with horror that it was going to get one final blow in before it died.

It crashed into the ground in the middle of a line of Capitol Police. The propeller swung like scythes, and Jess cried out and covered her eyes with her hands.

Jake didn't turn away. He made himself watch. He made sure to memorize the faces of all nine police officers who sacrificed their lives as the drone crashed into the ground.

The motorcade proceeded safely away. The Vice President was safe.

But it had come at the cost of dozens of law enforcement officers.

A hush fell over the control room, broken only by the equally subdued voices of the team leads as they reported their various spheres of responsibility were secure.

When they finished, Jake sighed. "All right," he said. "Let's get everything cleaned up and get everyone home."

Everyone who could get home, at least.

Jake surveyed the damage, blood boiling.

They would pay. If it was the last thing he did, he would make sure that all of the people responsible for this were brought to justice.

CHAPTER NINE

"You need rest, Jake. You haven't slept in almost thirty-six hours."

Jake frowned at Jess. "We've all been pulling long hours. I can't leave when there's still work to be done."

"We've all found time to rest during these long hours. Everyone except you."

"I'll be fine."

"Fine isn't good enough, Jake."

Jake's frown deepened, but he met an equally hard gaze from Jess. "The longer you go without sleep, the less effective you'll be. We can't afford for you to be anything less than one hundred percent effective, so go home and *sleep*. That's an order."

"You're not my superior."

"Don't argue with me. You know I'm right."

Jake met her gaze a moment longer, but finally, he sighed and lowered his eyes. She *was* right. He could handle long stretches without sleep on occasion, but since the Lincoln Memorial attack, he had pulled three all-nighters and enjoyed less than three hours of sleep every other night. He could feel his mind starting to slow, and as Jess said, they needed him at one hundred percent.

"You're right. I'll go get some shuteye. I'm back here at six tomorrow morning, though."

"Eight."

"Six. Quit while you're ahead."

She sighed, then said more softly. "Okay. Six. And don't worry. We're the best in the business. We'll hold down the fort while you're recuperating."

Jess and two dozen other analysts were poring over footage and data trying to determine the origin of the drone and to find a clue to who was operating it. They would continue to review data until they were confident of the answers to those questions.

"I know you will," he said. "I'll see you tomorrow."

He headed home, trying and failing to keep his worries from overwhelming him.

Trident had seen and exploited the one weakness in Jake's security setup.

No, they hadn't seen it and exploited it. They hadn't been opportunistic. They had planned for that event and prepared well for it. They had known ahead of time that Jake wouldn't consider an aerial assault. They had that drone built, programmed, and waiting for something they knew was going to occur even before Jake did.

Maybe it was just his fatigue talking, but he thought the key was the man who remained unidentified from the Lincoln Memorial attack. Whoever was running Trident's show not only had access to excellent weaponry but also seemed well versed in Secret Service procedures. Trident had failed to assassinate the President and Vice President, but both attacks had resulted in significant civilian loss of life.

Jake reached his apartment feeling as close to defeated as he ever had in his life. The only other time he had felt this way was after the single botched operation in his entire military career. Not the one where he had disobeyed orders but the one where he had followed them to disastrous effect.

He headed to his door, and he must truly be exhausted because he didn't notice Sheila standing in front of it until he was halfway up the stairs. "Sheila. What's going on?"

She smiled and said, "Nothing much. I just wanted to see you to see how you were doing."

"Where's Special Agent Trent?"

"He's in the car." She blushed a little. "I asked him to wait outside."

Jake felt heat climb his cheeks. They were both adults. She had come to his apartment at night to check on him. She wasn't here just to see how he was doing.

Relax, Jake. You're tired. Take it at face value and stop trying to infer meaning where there is none meant.

"Thank you. I appreciate that."

They stood in awkward silence for a moment before Sheila said, "So… can I come in?"

She definitely meant something.

"Sure. Of course. I mean… sorry, I'm tired. Come on in."

"It's all right. You've been working hard. I won't keep you for very long."

"Take as long as you need," he said.

He opened the door and led the two of them inside. All at once, he was embarrassed about his apartment. It wasn't messy, but it was spartan. The living room consisted of a sofa, a tv and a coffee table.

The dining room was one square table with four chairs. There were no decorations anywhere to be seen, and in the event that they did end up in his bedroom, she would see only a basic bedframe and box spring underneath his mattress and a single dresser. It was a typical bachelor pad, he supposed, but he wasn't a college kid, he was a thirty-five-year-old adult.

Keep it together.

"Would you like something to drink?" he asked.

"No, thank you," she said. "I just…" She bit her lip, and Jake yearned for her. "I just wanted to thank you. I know you've been working really hard to keep my father safe, and I really appreciate it."

"It's my job," he replied with a smile. "I'm happy to do it."

She nodded. "Do you know if Francis is all right?"

"The Vice President? She's fine. She's at a secure location right now. Chafing to be let loose just like Bry—like your father was. But she's fine."

"That's good. She's a tough old shrew, but she's got a good heart."

Hearing the Vice President referred to as a tough old shrew drew a laugh from Jake. Sheila joined him, and he was struck once more by the beauty of her voice.

"Would you like to sit?" he asked, gesturing to the couch.

"Thank you," Sheila replied.

She sat in the middle of the couch, meaning that wherever Jake sat, he would be right next to her. She looked expectantly up at him, and he stood awkwardly a moment longer, trying and failing to get control of his pounding heart.

This was wrong. This was stupid. This was dangerous. He considered Bryan a friend, but the truth was he was more of an acquaintance than a friend. They had a good relationship, but at the end of the day, Sheila's father was the President of the United States, and he was a Secret Service agent assigned to protect him. That trumped any friendship they might share and precluded any romantic possibility with Sheila. Besides, friends didn't want their friends to sleep with their daughters.

He thought of his earlier speculation about ending up in the bedroom and reddened.

Sheila noticed his discomfort and smiled. "Are you going to sit with me?"

Oh yes. She absolutely intended for tonight to end in the bedroom.

And Jake knew that no amount of willpower would be enough to resist her.

He resigned himself to his fate and sat next to her. She took his hand in hers and ran her fingers through his. They didn't say anything for a moment. When they did speak, Sheila began.

"I don't think these guys are going to stop. Whoever they are, I think they want more than just a few scares. That drone wasn't necessary if all they wanted was to stir the pot. They wanted Francis dead."

"Yes," Jake said. "I agree. We believe that the group responsible intends to assassinate your father and won't stop until that aim is accomplished."

"How do we stop them?"

"The easiest way would be to convince your father not to run for reelection."

She laughed. "You and I both know he won't pull out of the race."

"And he shouldn't. We can't let people believe that terrorists can have this kind of effect on the President."

She smiled with a touch of bitterness. "You sound just like my father."

He deflated a little. "I know. He just happens to be right in this case."

She turned one of his hands over palm up and traced her fingers up and down his arm to the elbow. Her face seemed pensive, and he wasn't sure if she was aware of the movement or if it was just an unconscious attempt to comfort herself. Either way, it sent shivers all through his body.

"How can you make that promise?" she asked out of nowhere.

"I'm sorry?"

"You promised you wouldn't let anything happen to him or to me. How can you keep that promise?"

Jake fought the frown that wanted to come to his face. The hard truth of the matter was that he couldn't guarantee that. He could guarantee that he would do everything in his power to protect them, and in fact, that was exactly what he had said.

That wasn't the same as guaranteeing he would succeed, though, and that was the guarantee Sheila wanted. He understood that, but he also understood that as unlikely as it was, there was always a slim chance that someone would get lucky, some bullet would make it through, some bomb would go off at just the right time.

He debated his response, but in the end decided honesty was the best policy. "I can guarantee that I and everyone else in the Secret Service will fight to the death to protect you. I can guarantee that we have the tools and training necessary to provide an incredibly high likelihood of success. I can guarantee that we will not stop until every single person responsible for these attacks is brought to justice."

"But you can't promise me that we'll be safe. Not with absolute certainty."

He hated the words that left his mouth now, but they were the truth, and she deserved that. "No, ma'am. Not with absolute certainty."

She gave him an odd smile. "Why do you call me ma'am?"

"Because you're the President's daughter, and it's my job to protect you."

"But you also call me Sheila."

"Yes, ma—Sheila. At your request, I call you by your first name whenever I can remember to do so."

"And you hold my hand and let me caress your arm. You embrace me and hold me like a lover. Do you do all of those things to protect me too?"

Time seemed to stop for Jake. His senses sharpened as the crucial moment finally arrived. This was the time he could resist. This was his chance to stop whatever was growing between them before it was too strong. This was when he could do the right thing and not only protect his job but protect Sheila from potential embarrassment.

Instead, he kissed her.

It happened so fast he wasn't even aware of it until he felt her lips part to kiss him back. He felt her stiffen and gasp, then almost immediately melt into him and pull him close as though afraid he would pull away if she let him.

It was too late for that. There was no pulling away anymore. Right or wrong, the two of them would be lovers, and Jake would face whatever consequences awaited him for that decision.

Her hand slid to his waistband and closed, grabbing a fistful of his shirt so she could lift it over his head.

And his phone rang.

He pulled away, and for a crystal-pure moment, he hated whoever was on the other end of that phone call with more intensity than he had ever hated anything in his life.

Then he saw Art's name, and reason asserted itself. "I'm sorry," he told Sheila. "It's my boss."

"Dad?"

"No, Art, uh, Director Davis."

He answered. "Mercer. What is it?"

"Jake, I need you in my office ASAP. Where are you?"

Jake tensed. "I'm home, sir. My team requested that I rest so I could be fully capable of—"

"Yeah, that'll have to wait. You and I need to address something immediately."

Art had never used that tone with him before. Whatever they needed to address, it had pissed Art off to no end.

"I'm on my way, sir."

"On the double, Mercer."

He had never called Jake by his last name before either.

Jake turned reluctantly to Sheila and said, "I'm sorry. I…"

"It's okay," she said quickly. "This was probably a mistake anyway. I'm sorry I put you in this position."

"Don't be sorry," he said, stifling the stab he felt in his heart. "It was flattering to know that you thought of me like this."

She smiled wryly at him, and he said, "I mean. I just meant that I enjoyed—"

She rescued him from making more of a fool of himself by standing and kissing him softly again. This kiss was far more chaste than the first, but it carried just as much emotion. "Go talk to your boss, Jake. Thank you for making me feel safe."

He met her eyes and yearned to say what he knew he couldn't say.

But instead, he just said, "Of course, Sheila."

CHAPTER TEN

"With the passing of fifty-eight-year-old Fatima Housiman this evening, the death toll from the attack on Wednesday has now climbed to thirty. While many of the victims were law enforcement agents acting to defend the Vice President from the surprise drone attack, several, including Housiman, were civilians hoping simply to enjoy a chance to honor those who fell in the devastating terrorist attacks that struck our nation over twenty years ago.

Now Housiman's family, and a shocked and mournful nation, are left to wonder how such a damaging attack could have occurred, especially only one week after the bombing of the Lincoln Memorial left six people dead."

The news feed switched to images of the Lincoln Memorial attack, including a thirty-second clip of coroner wagons loading the bodies of the slain onto gurneys. Jake looked at Art, who stood behind his desk with a stony frown on his face. "Art, this is just sensationalist bullshit. It sucks, but this is what they always—"

"Shut up and watch."

Jake bristled at the rudeness, but he refrained from firing back at his boss and turned his attention back to the tv. A pundit who labeled himself a "security expert" based on his three years of experience flying a desk at Fort Irwin argued that the deaths rested squarely on the shoulders of the Secret Service.

"They insisted on taking the lead on this. If they do that, then they need to be prepared for whatever threat they might face. Considering we live in a world where anyone can buy a drone for two hundred dollars at a department store, it's utterly unbelievable and unacceptable that the Secret Service didn't plan for that possibility."

Jake felt heat climb his cheeks. The drones you could buy for a hundred ninety-nine at Walmart were a far cry from the machine that caused the attack two days ago, and they had no reason to believe someone would actually be able to fly a half-ton drone armed with an anti-material machine gun into the National Mall. The pundit, as usual, was talking out of his ass. He probably hadn't even written his own talking points.

The pundit disappeared, replaced once more by the anchor. "*In light of the recent tragedy, people have begun to ask who could be responsible for this heinous crime.*"

Jake would have expected any number of outlandish claims to be brought forward. He would have anticipated anything but to see his own face show up immediately after that sentence. His eyes widened in shock, and he listened, first with anger, then with disgust, then with fear as the anchor said, "*Sources have informed this network that the person responsible for the safety of the Vice President and the attendees at the Remembrance Day Parade was this man, Senior Special Agent Jacob Mercer of the Secret Service.*

"According to the Secret Service, Jacob Mercer has been a role model agent, effective, driven and possessed of an outstanding work ethic and commitment to his job. But a look under the surface reveals a troubling past that has many questioning whether he should be allowed to have any authority at all."

The scene changed to show stock footage of the fighting in the Middle East from around ten years ago. *"According to an anonymous source, when Jacob Mercer was a Marine Corps sniper deployed to the volatile Kandahar region in Afghanistan, he led an operation to kill a terrorist leader believed to be tangentially connected to the infamous terrorist attacks that spawned the holiday on which Fatima Housiman and twenty-nine others were killed. During this operation, then Staff Sergeant Mercer botched his assigned duties and alerted the terrorists to the presence of the joint assault team. As a result of this mistake, six Marines were killed. Mercer was eventually acquitted of wrongdoing by a court-martial, but questions about his effectiveness have lingered to this day."*

Art reached for the remote on his desk and shut the television off. He glared at Jake, and Jake said, "Sir, I don't know who they talked to, but they have very incomplete information."

"Well, let me tell you who I talked to," Art said.

He reached inside his desk drawer and pulled out a file, dropping it onto the desk. Jake glanced at the heading and saw it was the official debriefing for the incident referenced on the news.

"I'll save you some discomfort by telling you that I already read it," Art said. "Boy did it hurt my eyes."

"Sir, if you'll let me explain—"

"I don't need you to justify your actions here," Art said, tapping the file. "That's between you and the Corps. They satisfied themselves that you did everything you could, so it doesn't really matter what my personal opinion is."

Jake's lips thinned. "What is your personal opinion, sir?"

"That I should have known about this during your interview process."

Jake felt a knife through his gut. Art must have noticed that in his expression because he said, "Any reason why you didn't mention this?"

"The court-martial was sealed, sir. I didn't believe the incident was relevant to my job here at the Secret Service."

"How do you feel now?"

"I still feel it's not relevant. What does a military operation from ten years ago have anything to do with what I do for the Service now?"

"I'll tell you what. It makes you a media liability. The nation is angry, Jake. They're looking for someone to blame, and you just gave them someone. It doesn't matter if it's stupid. It doesn't matter if it's wrong. It's satisfying. A lot of scared and upset civilians don't have to feel scared and upset anymore. 'It's not dangerous. If they had put someone competent in charge, everyone would have been fine. This guy's just an idiot, and so is the Secret Service for putting him in charge.'"

"Do you feel that way, sir?"

"I feel that you're missing the point, Jake. What I feel would have mattered before Wednesday. What I feel would have been important if I had known about this"—he tapped the file—"before I made you the face of this investigation. We could have had a plan in place, Jake. We could have had talking points to address this event and assure people that you were more than capable of leading this investigation and keeping the Vice President and the public safe."

"It's not my job to keep the public safe, sir."

"Would you like me to tell them that? When Channel Four news calls and asks, 'Hey, Art, why did you put an idiot in charge?' would you like me to respond, 'Well, he's not an idiot anymore, and anyway, it's not his job to care about civilians. He's got better things to do.'?"

Jake didn't respond.

Art sighed and slumped back into his desk. "I just don't get why you didn't tell me. We could have worked through this."

"If I had revealed this to you, would I have a job with this agency?" Jake asked.

Art didn't reply for a long time. Finally, he sighed and said, "We can do damage control. It's going to be a hell of a ride, but I can get us through the media circus. People are afraid right now, but as the fear calms down, they'll start to think again, and we can leverage that to remind them that the blame lies with the terrorists, not those trying to combat the terrorists."

"I'll do whatever you need me to do, sir."

"I need you as far from the media as you can get. I need you to be so news-phobic that the sight of a Channel Four van sends you shrieking in terror to the Catacombs. You let *me* handle the media, and you don't say a damned word to them. Do you understand?"

"Yes, sir."

"Outstanding. The second thing I need from you is everything."

"Sir?"

"Everything. Every single damned thing. Everything you've ever done that could possibly come to reflect poorly on you or the Secret Service. Ever run a red light? I need to know. Ever refuse to tip a waitress? I need names and dates. Ever screw a drunk politician? I need their names too."

Jake thought about the kiss he had shared with Sheila only minutes ago and felt a fresh stab of guilt.

"Anything, Mercer? You're quiet. I don't like quiet."

"No, sir," he said. "Nothing."

Art met his eyes and said nothing for a long time. Jake forced himself to maintain eye contact even as his heart pounded in his chest. Finally, Art sighed. "All right. I believe you. I hope I don't have to explain what's going to happen to you if I find out you're a liar."

"No, sir," Jake said. "I understand."

"Wonderful." Art put the file away and stared pensively ahead for a moment before turning back to Jake.

"There's going to be an internal investigation too."

Jake frowned. "So this does impact my position with the agency."

"Most likely not."

"Most *likely* not? Sir…" he composed himself. "Art, please be honest with me."

That was a mistake. Art frowned and said darkly, "Don't you dare talk to me about honesty right now, Jake. Don't you fucking dare?"

Jake pressed his lips together and remained silent.

After a moment, Art continued. "There has to be an internal investigation, Jake. We can't have this kind of media exposure during this kind of crisis and have the man in charge of addressing this crisis revealed to have this kind of past without some sort of attempt at accountability." Jake began to protest, and Art lifted his hand. "Again, it doesn't matter how I feel about anything. This is what's best for the Agency."

"And if Internal Affairs determines I'm no longer fit for duty, sir?"

"Then this nation will suffer greatly due to your decision to hide information from me."

Jake clammed up again.

"I strongly doubt that will happen. There's nothing in this file that would justify terminating or even reassigning you. However, it will help a lot if by the time the investigation concludes, you have some good news for me. So, if I were you, I would do whatever it takes to get me some good news. Find these assholes, Jake. Do whatever you can. Give the nation someone to look at other than you. Do that, and it won't matter what mistakes you may have made."

Jake could have refuted every single point Art had made, but it was clear his boss wasn't interested in hearing him right now. So, he just nodded and said, "Yes, sir."

"Good. Dismissed. Now, go home and do what your team told you to do. Get some rest, put the circus out of your mind, and come back in the morning ready to work. Understood?"

"Yes, sir."

"Outstanding."

Jake's feelings alternated between numb and angry as he made his way back home. Who had tipped them off? Could someone in the Corps have seen a chance at fifteen minutes of fame?

Or did Trident somehow have access to his background?

And what if they found out about him and Sheila?

He reached his apartment to find Sheila gone. He wasn't surprised to feel relief and disappointment at the same time.

His phone buzzed. He sighed and opened his phone, expecting another message from Art or maybe from Sheila.

The text was instead from a private number. Jake read it, and his blood boiled.

Having fun yet?

CHAPTER ELEVEN

The night's sleep left Jake in a somewhat better mood. He still didn't feel wonderful about the media circus that now surrounded him, but at least it hadn't progressed to the point where vans waited outside to surround him and pepper him with questions when he left.

He showered and made himself a breakfast of eggs and bacon, then dressed for work. He would arrive at the office at five forty-five, fifteen minutes early. Enough time to make coffee for himself and sugared cream seasoned with coffee for Jess.

He felt another touch of fear when he thought of Jess. The two of them had worked together for years, but she knew very little of his past. How would she react when she learned about what was in the news right now?

Well, there was nothing left to do but face it. He sighed and reminded himself that all that was important right now was protecting the President and Sheila.

He opened the door and realized immediately that Jess's opinion of him was the least of his worries. Sheila stood in his doorway, and she was pissed.

"Sheila," he began, "What—"

She put a hand on his chest and pushed him back into the apartment, then followed and shut the door. Normally, Jake wouldn't let anyone handle him like that, but he was too surprised and hurt to do anything other than stare at her in shock.

She lifted her cell phone, which showed an article of the news story that had aired the night prior. "What the hell is this?" she asked.

He blinked and struggled to recover his composure. "That has nothing to do with you or your father or my job with the Service."

"Don't you dare be coy with me. Dammit, Jake, I trusted you! I kissed—"

She pressed her lips together and looked away. Jake had thought he had suffered the worst pain any man could suffer, but when he heard her remorse at their kiss he realized there was worse pain still. "I'm sorry for that," he said. "I should never have kissed you. It was inappropriate and irresponsible, and it won't happen again."

"*This* is inappropriate and irresponsible," she retorted, lifting the phone again. "Does Dad know?"

"No, and he doesn't need to."

She scoffed. "Doesn't *need* to? Well, I sort of think he does, Jake, since you're the person in charge of making sure he, I and Mom don't die. I think he absolutely needs to know what sort of person you are."

That finally broke Jake's façade. "What sort of person I am, Sheila, is the sort of person who repeatedly and unquestioningly puts his own life in danger, along with the lives of friends and colleagues I respect, for the sole purpose of keeping you and your family alive. I have been working tirelessly to find the people responsible for these attacks. Last night was the first night of full rest I've had in a week. I've chased suspects through the city, I've found evidence and analyzed it, and I've coordinated the efforts of a half-dozen agencies and hundreds of law enforcement and security officers to work together to bring these terrorists to justice.

"What you're reading is a news network's sensationalist retelling of an event they have absolutely no understanding of. That is a misrepresentation of who I am, but even worse, it's a misrepresentation of men and women who laid down their lives to keep this country and the world safe from assholes like the people who tried to kill your father. No one has any right to besmirch their memories, and I won't stand it from anyone, not even you."

Sheila shrank back a little, and Jake lowered his voice. "If you'd like, I can explain my side of the events referred to in that article. Then you can make your own decision as to what sort of person I am."

Sheila nodded. "I would like that. Thank you."

"Okay. Would you like to sit?"

Sheila nodded and sat on the far right side of the couch. Jake felt a pang but took the hint and sat on the far left side, leaving as much distance as possible between the two of them. "Okay," he said, "I'm about to tell you things I've never told anyone, so I'd appreciate if they remained in this room. Can you keep this between us?"

She nodded again. "Of course."

"Okay." He sighed and steeled himself for what he knew would be a very uncomfortable trip down memory lane.

"Ten years ago, I was assigned to a SEAL team to take out Ahsan Abdullah."

"Who's Ahsan Abdullah?"

"He was suspected of partially funding Al-Qaeda back when Al-Qaeda was just a small-time group. He had cut ties with Al-Qaeda before 9/11, but he was known to be involved with other militant terrorist groups in Central Asia. The CIA got a tip that he was planning a terrorist attack in Hong Kong and assigned us to take him out before he could succeed.

"So, we flew into Afghanistan and waited. He was in Tajikistan in hiding, but we knew he would have to travel to Afghanistan to recruit freedom fighters because the Tajiki government was very clear that he was not allowed to recruit their citizens. We waited for three weeks then got word that he was going to cross the border under cover of night."

He took a deep breath. The next part was painful for him. "I was sent ahead with one of the SEALs to scout for any ambushes he might be setting for us along the way. We didn't see anything, so we called the team to wait."

"And there was an ambush?"

"Yes. Somehow, Abdullah caught wind of our operation and secretly bribed village leaders to set a trap for us. They didn't set it beforehand, which is why we knew nothing of us." He took a breath. "Basically, they waited until we left our outpost, then followed us. We were scheduled to be in position to take Abdullah out an hour before he arrived. The ambush arrived ten minutes before Abdullah."

Sheila gasped. "And they killed those men?"

"They had almost three hundred on their side, and they got the drop on us. We mowed them down like… well, we were winning, but by the time the fighting stopped, there were only two of us left."

"Oh my God. Did you get Abdullah?"

Jake savored the look of fright in Abdullah's face as the terrorist leader's smile vanished. He waited a split second longer to allow Abdullah to process his doom. Then he thrust with the knife.

"I did."

Jake fell silent, the quiet as thick as a blanket in between the two of them. Sheila leaned back and crossed her arms, a typical defensive measure that people used when they were unsure or uncomfortable.

Jake waited patiently for her to speak. He had shared his piece. It was up to her to decide whether to believe him or not.

Finally, Sheila said, "I'm sorry for what happened to you, Jake. I can't imagine how hard it must have been for you to see your brothers and sisters killed like that."

"No," Jake said, "you can't."

He didn't intend for his words to be accusatory, but he couldn't quite stifle that emotion. Sheila stiffened slightly and lowered her eyes.

"I'm still not happy that you hid this from the Secret Service, though. Why did you do that?"

Because a part of me still hates myself for it.

"Because it wasn't related to my job," he said out loud. "I didn't feel it was representative of the talents I bring to the agency, and it certainly doesn't reflect poorly on my character."

Sheila kept her gaze averted, and her head lowered. Part of Jake wanted to apologize and tell her that everything was okay, and she didn't need to feel guilty. Another part of her was still angry at the fact that once more people were seeing him in a different light.

A failure.

Another part of him was forced to admit that she had a good point. His job was to protect the President and his family. No personal consideration was more important than that task. He had no right to value his own peace of mind over the integrity of his job.

He took a breath and said, "I apologize for not disclosing this information. You're right. It should have come up regardless of my feelings on the subject."

Sheila didn't reply for a while. She sat where she was, staring at her fidgeting fingers. Jake wished he could be a million miles away right now.

Finally, she sighed and said, "Thank you for your apology. For the time being, I support your continued position as a senior member of our security detail. You've done an exemplary job of that."

The forced formality of her tone cut Jake deeply. She made no attempt to hide her anger, letting every drop of venom show through her terse speech.

Jake guessed at the source of her anger. "Listen, Sheila… if you're afraid this will come back to you in any way…"

He guessed wrong. Her eyes snapped to him in shock, and before he could backpedal from the point, she said, "Excuse me? You lied to your superior to get a job protecting me and my family, and you think I'm upset because we *kissed?"*

Jake didn't know what to say, so he offered a rather weak "I'm sorry."

Sheila shook her head. "Jake, you're a good Secret Service Agent, but I'm beginning to wonder what your motives were for taking this job."

Anger surfaced again. "My motive is to protect the President of the United States and his family, *ma'am.* And I will continue to execute that duty with the utmost focus and dedication."

Sheila pursed her lips together and nodded. After a moment, she met his eyes and said, "All right. Thank you for talking to me. I'll see you later, Special Agent Mercer."

She left his apartment, and he sighed and swore softly before heading to the living room and collapsing on the couch.

The entire exchange had been rather childish. Both of them were allowing their anger to get to them, and it was affecting their behavior.

The problem was that he didn't get to make those mistakes. He didn't have the right to be emotional about anything related to his job. The entire point of the Secret Service was to make sure that nothing got in the way of the President's safety. There was no room for anything else.

But he had still lied.

He was still emotional.

He wasn't the right man for this job. He could protect the President without allowing emotion into the equation. He couldn't protect the President, investigate an assassination attempt, and develop a romantic attachment with the President's daughter and keep his emotions under control.

He would have to ask Art to—

His phone rang. Jess.

"Yeah."

"Jake, you need to come here. We have some information on the case."

"What is it?"

She paused a moment. "I think you'd better come see this in person."

He sighed and checked the time. Another sleepless night.

"I'm on my way."

As he dressed and rode to the office, he realized it was too late to back out. Right or wrong, the case had progressed too far under his leadership to be placed in anyone else's hands. He would need to keep things together long enough to catch the people who had tried to assassinate the President. After that, he could make a decision about whether or not he wished to remain with the Service.

Suck it up, Marine.

Jake smiled slightly at Max's voice in his conscience. "I'll do my best, Master Gunny."

CHAPTER TWELVE

Jake stared at the image on the screen and wished desperately that he was having a nightmare.

"We're sure of this?"

"He was the sixth man at the Lincoln Memorial assassination," Jess confirmed. "The data on the radio confirms that. He was the architect of the bombing."

Jake felt as though a knife were driven into his gut. He sat calmly in his chair, his arms resting lightly on the desk, but though his body was relaxed, his mind was screaming in pain.

Drew? It couldn't be. Drew was a patriot. Drew loved America. He fought for its freedom and for its institutions. There was no way he could be the one behind an assassination attempt.

Corporal Andrew McNeill was Jake's best friend in the Marine Corps. The two men met just after boot camp at sniper school. Both had gone on to become premier marksmen, although halfway through sniper school, Drew switched to Gunnery school and became a machine gun operator.

It didn't make any sense. Even considering what had happened to Drew, Jake couldn't believe that he was the man behind these attacks.

But someone had texted him last night. Jake had a different number than he had before, but who else would want to single him out specifically?

"Have you found anything out about the text I got?" Jake asked. "Could it have been Drew who sent it?"

"I don't know. The text came from a burner phone."

He sighed. "So there's no way to tell."

"Not unless we happen to stumble across the phone."

He sighed. "All right. May I see the decrypted messages from the radio?"

Jess wordlessly handed the printout of the messages to Jake. In the three years he had known her, this was the first time she had ever looked truly sad.

Jake read through the messages, and all protests died in his heart. Not only was Drew mentioned by name, but his mannerisms and style were evident in his communications.

Jake took a deep breath, and when he exhaled, he found some semblance of control. “All right. Reach out to the FBI and let them know we have the identity of the final suspect. Add him to the manhunt list and put an APB out on any vehicles he’s been known to use.”

“I’ve done all that,” Jess said, “but Jake… there’s something else you should know.”

Jake met Jess’s eyes. “What could possibly be worse than this?”

“Well, I don’t know about worse, but it’s still bad.”

Jake sighed and rubbed his eyes. “Tell me.”

“We’ve identified another key actor in Trident. We believe he’s the new head of the organization and the shot-caller behind both attacks.”

“I thought you said Drew was the shot-caller at the Lincoln Memorial.”

“We believe he planned that particular attack, but we believe another individual is the one organizing the string of terrorist attacks in Washington, D.C.”

“I’m afraid to ask who, but who?”

Jess sighed and clicked a link on the screen. When Jake saw the next image to pop up, He laughed bitterly and rubbed his eyes again. “Oh man. How awesome is that? Two traitors at the same time. What a damned miracle.”

“I’m sorry, Jake. This one’s personal for me too.”

This one was none other than former Secret Service Special Agent Eli Bard. Special Agent Bard was at one point the most celebrated agent within the Secret Service. He wasn’t well-known publicly, since the Secret Service preferred that their agents weren’t known publicly, but within the agency, he was the celebrity superstar.

Despite this fame, he had left the agency on rather less than amicable terms after making statements that seemed to support certain terrorist activities. That was the official story, anyway. Jake was one of very few people who knew that Bard’s actions went far beyond speech.

And now it seemed he had graduated to full-on terrorism. And he had recruited Jake’s best friend into his fold.

Jess showed him another printout indicating that Drew referred to Bard as Chief and that he deferred to him for permission to begin the assassination attempt. The other already named suspects deferred to both men. It looked like Drew was Bard’s senior lieutenant.

Why? Jake didn't understand it. What did they hope to accomplish? Did they think the world was going to change just because they acted like fools? Were people supposed to respect them now that they had killed civilians in their pursuit of a political statement?

The more he thought about it, the more anger overcame his grief. These men had betrayed their oaths. They had acted specifically to destroy the institutions they were sworn to protect.

And they would suffer the consequences.

"I do have one piece of good news." Jess told him. "I was able to decrypt an address."

Jake's ears perked up. "An address for one of the suspects?"

"We're not sure. Not a primary residence, but it's possible that one or more of the suspects resides there. It's an abandoned warehouse in Capitol Heights, Maryland. It used to belong to a bookseller, but a private company bought the property fifteen years ago."

"What company?"

"EB Holdings."

"EB as in Eli Bard?"

"Well, not officially, but one can assume that since we now know that Trident has been meeting there."

"So it's like their hideout?"

"Looks that way."

"Wonderful. Can I see the address?"

Jess showed him the address, and Jake copied it into his cell phone. "Perfect. I know it's a lot to ask, Jess, but how do you feel about working overtime?"

"Oh, I don't sleep. I just put an IV into my arm and freebase coffee when I need to juice up."

"Please don't ever use the term freebase around me again."

"Shoot up? Take a bump? Take a hit?"

Jake rolled his eyes and said, "I'm going to reconnoiter the hideout tonight."

Jess's mischievous smile vanished. "What?"

"I know you heard me."

"Yeah, I heard you, I'm just giving you a chance to think clearly. Are you serious? You can't go there alone."

"I won't. You'll be with me." He tapped his earpiece.

"No, this is not a good idea. Jake, we can have a team together in less than an hour. Let me call Art and—"

"No."

"Why not?"

"Because I don't want to show our hand just yet. If I go alone, I can check out the camp unseen. I can ensure that we're correct about Trident's leadership, and we can prepare an appropriate response at that time."

"The appropriate response is to show up with overwhelming force. You're a Marine, and you understand that."

"You aren't a Marine, and you don't know what you're talking about."

Jess blinked and stepped back. Jake felt a rush of guilt. He had never spoken so dismissively to her before. He sighed. "I'm sorry, Jess. Look, I need you to trust me on this, okay? I know that this is a risk. I know it's against protocol. But if we show up like the Marines would and blow everything up, we might just force them underground. If we act like special agents and gather all pertinent information before we act, then we can determine the appropriate response, one that will ensure that Trident is no longer able to operate within the United States."

"We're Secret Service Special Agents," Jess reminded him. "Not FBI."

Jake sighed again. "Please, Jess. Please just trust me."

She didn't answer him right away. When she finally spoke, she said, "All right, Jake. But you need to keep yourself together. I'm starting to worry about you."

"I'll be fine. I know what I'm doing."

***

One hour later, Jake arrived at the warehouse. He parked across the street behind another warehouse and approached the building on foot from the other side.

He heard voices as he approached the building. They spoke in low tones, but as Jake reached the building, he could begin to identify different voices. One of them he recognized as Barnes. Another he recognized as Drew.

A third voice that he didn't recognize was speaking now. "…able to evade him the first time. I'm confident I can do so again."

That must be Gunnar Jefferson. Barnes replied to his assertion with, "It's not just Mercer you need to think about. A lot of people say you playing around on that sports bike. Not to mention, your face is on a surveillance video."

"All of our faces are on surveillance videos. Isak and Walter still go to the same coffee shop every morning, and no one bats an eye. That's why we were chosen. We look like everyone else."

"Isak and Walter don't lead Secret Service agents on wild bike chases," Drew pointed out.

"Well, what was I supposed to do? Let him catch me?"

"That would have been better than making yourself a TV star."

"Jake?" Jess said, "I'm sending backup. We have what we need now."

"All right," Jake said, "Go ahead."

Then he heard Bard's voice. "All right. I think we've made our point. For the time being, Gunnar, you are to keep a low profile. I'll reach out to Isak and Walter and make sure they do the same. Let's head home for tonight, and when LeShaun gets back from Manitoba, we can move forward with Operation Three."

Jake tapped his earpiece. "Jess, how long until backup arrives?"

"The team will be there in an hour."

Jake swore under his breath. "That's not enough time. I'm going in."

"What? Jake, no."

"They're leaving now, Jess. We'll lose our chance to capture them if we hesitate."

"Jake, you are *one man.* You can't take three probably armed terrorists by yourself."

"Watch me."

"No! Jake!"

He rushed into the building, diving through the window and rolling to his knees with his gun drawn. The shocked faces of Eli Bard, Andrew McNeill and Gunnar Jefferson stared his way.

Eli looked much the same as Jake remembered: tall, somber and dignified. His hair was slightly grayer, and he had a full beard, but otherwise, he was easily recognizable as the celebrated agent whose alternative political views got him into trouble and put an ignominious end to an otherwise illustrious career.

Drew had changed greatly in the past ten years. His once boyishly handsome face was now lined and weathered, making him look older than his thirty-five years of age. His hair was long and unkempt, and he had a rough stubble that extended the full length of his neck.

The most shocking change was in his eyes. His blue eyes had always been enthusiastic and bright. Now they were wild and bloodshot. Jake didn't imagine the serious Bard would allow a drug addict to occupy a senior position in his terrorist organization, so Drew's mental health must have deteriorated significantly in the past decade.

None of that mattered now. These men had attempted to assassinate the President and the Vice President.

"You are under arrest," Jake said. "Place your hands on top of your head, and—"

Drew's hand moved like a blur. He fired a split second before Jake. The impact of Drew's bullet in Jake's shoulder knocked his aim off of true, and the bullet meant for Drew's shoulder instead planted itself in Bard's arm. The disgraced former agent cried out and fell backward.

Jake tried to aim at the fallen terrorist leader, but his right arm had been seriously weakened by the shot, and his hand fell. He switched his gun to his left hand, but by that time, Gunnar had drawn his own weapon and now fired it at Jake.

He dove behind a stack of pallets. Wood splinters sprayed over his face at the impact of the round, but he managed to avoid harm.

"Get Bard out of here!" Gunnar yelled. "I'll hold him off!"

Jake growled and dove out from behind the pallets, bringing his handgun to bear. He fired at Gunnar, but his left hand wasn't as good at shooting as his right, and the bullet went wide.

Gunnar's bullet went wide also, but he kept firing, forcing Jake back into cover.

"No!" Jake shouted. "Goddammit!"

He tried to flank around the pallets, but before he could get a steady aim on Gunnar, the door of the warehouse burst inward. Jake caught sight of Drew driving a massive heavy-duty pickup truck into the building. Gunnar leapt onto the back and fired two more shots, pinning Jake down and giving the outlaws time to escape.

"Dammit!" Jake said.

He tried to rush to his motorcycle, but his head begin to swim from loss of blood. He collapsed to the ground, and the last thing he was aware of was Jess's voice screaming his name.

CHAPTER THIRTEEN

"After examining all available evidence, this court-martial finds Corporal Andrew McNeill guilty of dereliction of duty."

"What?" Jake shouted. "That's bullshit!"

"Sergeant Mercer, at ease!" the bailiff, First Sergeant Janet Gilroy barked.

"But that's—"

"Sergeant Mercer, remain at ease, or you will be detained!"

Jake clammed up and glared angrily at the judge.

The judge, Colonel Ariela Sanchez, frowned at Jake, then turned her attention to the court. "This court does not find sufficient evidence that Corporal McNeill's actions contributed to the deaths of the aforementioned servicemembers, however, there is no excuse for Corporal McNeill's cowardice or his refusal to follow orders. His actions dishonor the United States Marine Corps. As a result of his actions, this court orders that Corporal McNeil be reduced in rank to E-1 and be dishonorably discharged from the United States Marine Corps."

Jake looked at Drew and found his friend staring hatefully at him. "Drew, I'm sorry," he called. "I didn't know this would happen."

"Sergeant Mercer, remove yourself from this court!" First Sergeant Gilroy commanded.

"I'm sorry," Jake said, "I'm so sorry."

Jake started slightly and opened his eyes. Light seared his vision, and he squinted and brought his hand to his face to shield himself. As his vision cleared, he found himself staring at two faces.

One of the faces was concerned, the other very angry.

Jess, the owner of the concerned face, took his hand in both of hers. "Hi, Jake. How are you feeling?"

"I've been better," Jake said.

His words slurred, and he wasn't sure if it was fatigue or intoxication of some sort. He felt groggy. He looked to his right and found an IV bag labeled morphine and decided it was intoxication.

"Okay. Listen, the doctor's going to hold you here for the next twenty hours. You've already been here for four. They said that the bullet missed major arteries, but there's a small tear in an intermediate vein that they had to sew up. They need you here to heal for a bit, and then they'll release you."

"All right," Jake said. He squeezed Jess's hands. "Thank you."

She bit her lip and lowered her eyes. A moment later, Art said, "I wouldn't thank her just yet, Jake. She might have enabled you to ruin your career, and frankly, her future is looking damned cloudy too."

The details of Jake's dream were still fresh in his mind, and that in addition to the medicine caused him to react emotionally. "That's not fair, sir. She was only following my instructions."

"You don't have the authority to instruct her, and she isn't obligated to follow your instructions. She chose to, and she will face the consequences of her actions. As will you. Special Agent Foster, will you give us the room, please."

Jess nodded, her shoulders stiff. "Yes, sir."

She squeezed Jake's hand, then left. When Jake was alone with his boss, Art said, "This is only the second time in my life I've gone from respecting one of my agents as much as I respect you to believing that you are a liability to the service."

"We have the names of the suspects," Jake said. "Bard is one of them."

"Yes, I know. As is your former companion, Andrew McNeill. Jess briefed us on the information she gleaned from the radio you picked up."

"Yes. Listen. They're planning another attack."

"We know. We also have the transcript of the call between you two when you illegally conducted a reconnaissance mission that then turned into an illegal attempt to arrest three suspects without approval from your superiors."

"Art, listen. I had them. I had them right there. What was I supposed to do? Let them go?"

"You didn't have them, Jake. They had you. That's why you're in the hospital hooked to a bag of morphine, and they're still at large. Here's what you don't have anymore—the location of their meeting place. Because I guarantee you, they'll never use that meeting place again. So instead of providing us valuable intel and giving us a chance to conduct an effective operation that could have resulted in the capture of the terrorists responsible for nearly assassinating the President and Vice President, we have another potential media circus precipitated by an agent who picked the absolute worst time in his career to implode.

“I gave you more responsibility, Jake. I had faith in you. I saw something in you that I thought was special, something that this entire agency could learn from. What the hell happened?”

Jake didn’t answer right away. Part of him wanted to defend himself, but what would be the point? He clearly wasn’t as ready to face the three terrorists as he thought he was. He acted outside of his comfort zone because he wasn’t patient enough to follow procedure. He was a sniper, not a SEAL, but he stormed into the building like he was an action hero and ended up nearly getting himself killed.

But one thing was absolutely true.

“Sir, if I’d followed procedure, we would have found that warehouse empty. Trident would have concluded its meeting and Bard, McNeill and Jefferson would already have been on their way home. We wouldn’t have confirmation that they are the individuals behind the assassination attempts, and we wouldn’t have confirmation of an imminent third attack, which, by the way, they are meeting to discuss tomor—er, today.”

“Where are they meeting?”

Jake opened his mouth, then closed it. He felt heat climb his cheeks, and Art said, “Exactly. I’ll give you the recon, Jake. If that was the only thing you’d done, I would have been willing to look the other way. You could have given us the information we needed, and we could have shown up today to arrest them with a full team of officers. Hell, we could have gotten the FBI involved. We could have had Capitol Police shut down the roadways. You and I could be talking about how we were going to make sure that Trident had no avenue of escape instead of talking about what the end of your service with the agency will look like. We could have gotten all of Trident, not just these three, which I feel compelled to point out we also didn’t get.”

Jake frowned. “The end of my service?”

Art sighed. He sat in a chair and leaned forward, shoulders slumped. “Yes, Jake. For God’s sake. How could it be any other way? Do you understand how big of a mistake you made? We had a chance to stop them, and you ruined it.”

Jake’s jaw tightened, but he kept his tone calm. “We don’t know that they were planning to meet at that warehouse. They could change their meeting locations to avoid detection.”

“Is that why Bard bought it fifteen years ago?”

“So we’ve confirmed that Bard is owner of EB Holdings?”

“Don’t try to change the subject. Yes, they *could* have been meeting somewhere else. They *could* have been meeting on the moon. They *could* have planned to throw rotten persimmons at the President, hoping he was allergic to them. They *could* have done fucking anything. There's literally no end to what *could* have happened."

"Art, listen—"

"Here's what *did* happen, Jake. You *did* choose to act on critical intelligence against the advice of your partner and without informing your team or your superiors of your intention. You *did* choose to then attempt to engage against a larger enemy force without so much as alerting your superiors of your intention to do so.

"We were an hour away, Jake. Yes, Bard and the others would have escaped this time, but you could have given us information that would have led to their capture. At the very least, you could have made things harder for them. And you very well could have given us something that would have led to their capture today.

"Instead, here we are. So tell me. What should I do? You're me, and I'm you. What is the appropriate response to this situation?"

Jake didn't answer right away. He knew what the book would tell Art to do. Regulation would require Art to remove Jake from active duty pending an internal affairs investigation that would find him guilty of a whole slew of violations and drum him completely out of the service. He would probably be able to avoid prison time, but he would never work for a federal agency again.

But looking at the situation another way, if he hadn't acted, there was a possibility that they would have learned nothing. They now had incontrovertible proof of the principles involved in these assassination attempts. They had a suspicious company that might be a Trident front. And now that Trident knew the Secret Service was pursuing them, they could choose to lay low and go dormant for a while, which served the primary purpose of keeping the President and his family safe.

"I think you should consider the value I bring to the Service, both in this instance and in all aspects of my service. I think you should recognize the opportunities my actions have provided and endorse them as an appropriate response to the severity of the situation."

This time, it was Art's turn to pause. He looked over Jake and stared pensively at the opposite wall. "You want me to endorse your actions. Jake, where does your loyalty lie?"

"My loyalty is to the President of the United States, sir. That trumps everything, including my loyalty to the standard operating procedures of the Secret Service."

"Including your loyalty to the President's daughter?"

Jake flinched at that, which was all the confirmation Art needed. "Come on, Jake. She's spent more time at your apartment than the White House the past few days. Multiple agents noticed the way you two acted around each other at Outpost Alpha when you were planning the President's return to the White House. We're not stupid. You've been sleeping with her."

"No," Jake insisted. "No, that has not happened."

"But it will."

Jake replayed the argument he and Sheila had just had, and said, "No, sir. I don't believe it will."

"You don't *believe* it will. But if Sheila comes over batting her baby blues and says, 'Gee, Jake, I'm sorry. Please forgive me,' you'll be all too happy to show her just how much you forgive her, won't you?"

Jake's shoulders tensed a little. "There's no need to speak rudely of her, sir."

"Jesus Christ." Art leaned back and stared up at the ceiling. He shook his head softly and said, "All right, Jake. Reasoning with you seems to be a waste of time, so I'm just going to tell you what's going to happen. You told me at the beginning of this investigation that you're not the right choice to lead it. I see now that you were correct to feel that way. Because you warned me beforehand of your lack of competence to lead an investigation, and I chose to ignore your request that the task be given to someone else, I feel personally responsible for the shitshow that has ensued as a result. So, you will be allowed to remain at your job. I will take over leadership of this investigation. From now on, you will be responsible for executing the specific tasks I give you and not a damned thing more. When we put a stop to Trident and bring the principals of these assassination attempts to justice, we'll revisit your future with the agency. Until then, you live to do what I tell you to do. One final point: you do not contact Sheila Jackson. At all. Understand?"

Jake could have spent hours going point by point and defending himself to Art, but he realized that would be pointless. He sighed and said, "Yes, sir."

"Outstanding. You'll be released tomorrow morning. I don't want to see your face until the following morning. That's an order."

"Yes, sir."

"Good." Art stood and headed for the door. Just before he left, he paused and turned back to Jake. "There's a light at the end of this tunnel, Jake, but you need to turn around and go the other way if you want to see it. Do you understand?"

Jake nodded. “I understand, sir.”
“Good. Speedy recovery.”

CHAPTER FOURTEEN

Jake spent the rest of his convalescence playing the events of the past two days over and over in his mind. He thought back from Sheila's first visit to his apartment to his choice to storm the Trident hideout and questioned every one of his decisions.

He didn't like the conclusions he came to.

It was utterly wrong of him to kiss Sheila. That was a completely foolish breach of professionalism on his part.

She had started it, it was true. She had made her intentions very clear when she visited him. She had made her desires obvious, and he had only given her what she had most definitely wanted.

But he should have been stronger than that. He should have been strong enough to refuse her advances. He was a Secret Service agent. He didn't get to have normal human weaknesses. He could whine all day long about the fact that he was only a man, and she had pursued him and not the other way around, but at the end of the day, it didn't matter. He was the one who was supposed to be better than other people. He had to be. His job demanded it.

As far as the reconnaissance, he still defended his decision. The three terrorists wouldn't have been there if he waited for a Rapid Response Team. He wouldn't have the information he had now if he hadn't gone when he did.

But to storm the building alone? That wasn't just against Secret Service Protocol. That was against the protocol of every law enforcement and military organization in the United States, not to mention common sense.

He knew that, so why did he rush them? Why did he make a rookie mistake and assault an enemy stronghold without backup? If he told his Marine self that he had done this, then Staff Sergeant Jake Mercer would berate him for being a fool, just as Art had.

Well, he didn't need to worry about making bad calls anymore. Art had ensured that he could make no calls anymore.

That glum thought stuck with him as he made his way home after being released from the hospital. When he arrived home, he checked his messages. The only message was from Jess. It was an animated image of a penguin holding a heart that said GET WELL SOON!

Nothing from Art and nothing from Sheila.

He sat on the couch for a while, not watching a daytime talk show that seemed unusually concerned with the fashion choices of a singer who had just turned old enough to drink legally. When sitting alone at home became too much, he showered and dressed, then headed for Max's bar. He had no idea how his mentor and friend would react to news of what happened, but if anyone could sympathize with his situation, Max could.

He reached the bar just after the lunch rush. Once more, the bar was empty save for Jake, Max, his niece and a few older patrons. Max greeted him with a smile when he came in, but his smile vanished when he saw Jake's expression. "Uh oh. Bad news?"

"Yeah, you could say that."

"Let me get Trish to watch the bar," Max said, "then you and I can go talk."

Max joined Jake at a table set apart from the rest of the bar a moment later. He offered Jake a drink, but Jake refused. He wasn't much of a drinker, but as upset as he was right now, there was too much of a risk that one drink would turn into several."

"So what's going on?" Max asked. "You look like you've just returned from deployment."

Jake chuckled. "You could say that."

"Talk to me."

Jake told Max about his encounter with Sheila and then his ill-fated attempt to reconnoiter and apprehend the Trident members. When Max asked them who the Trident members were, Jake frowned.

"Drew's one of them, Max. Corporal McNeill. My buddy from sniper school."

"Aw hell," Max said, "I remember him. He seemed like a good kid."

"Well, he's gone off the deep end," Max said. "He looked like a coke addict."

Max sighed. "I'm sorry, Jake. I know you feel partly responsible for what happened to him."

"Not really. Not anymore. I'm still pissed that the prosecuting JAG officer twisted my words, but that's not my fault. I just don't get it. I don't get how you go from loving your country as much as Drew seemed to love it to wanting to destroy it the way Drew wants to destroy it now."

Max nodded. He leaned back in his chair and looked over Jake's shoulder. "Did I ever tell you about Lieutenant Hannity?"

"Hannity? No, I don't think so."

Max nodded again. "Well, in Desert Storm, I was a Corporal in Lieutenant Hannity's platoon. For obvious reasons, lieutenants are not the most popular people in war zones. Placing people fresh out of school in charge of combat veterans with years of experience is an enduring example of foolishness that I really can't understand. But I digress.

"Hannity was one of the exceptions. He was driven, he was noble, he was hardworking, and he loved his men fiercely. We loved him too. I looked up to him. He was only three years older than me, but I saw him as more of a father than a brother. I would have gone to the ends of the Earth for him.

"Anyway, we served together for one tour, and after that, I was moved to a different unit. He and I fell out of contact. Two years later, I saw him again, and… well, I didn't recognize what I saw.

"He was a captain now. He must have done a few things right to get himself a company, so I can't say when he changed or what prompted it. I only know that when I saw him again, it was like the man I knew had died and someone completely different was living in his body."

Max paused and took a sip of his whiskey. He swirled it around in his mouth a moment before swallowing it and stared over Jake's shoulder, the same pensive, drawn expression on his face that he wore a moment ago. "I saw him threatening civilians."

Jake's eyes widened. "Really?"

"Really. I don't know for sure what set him off, and I don't know how serious he took the threats or how far he would have carried it. I only know that he had his gun pressed against the head of an Iraqi woman and was shouting at her that if she didn't respect him, he would blow her head off in front of her children."

"Jesus."

"Yeah. Not something you expect to walk into. Anyway, I leveled my rifle at him and ordered him to stand down. He looked up at me, and I saw so much hate in his eyes. It shocked me. He had always been strong and noble, but the man staring at me was ugly and lost and just… not the man I knew." He took a deep breath and continued. "He smiled at me a moment later, released the woman and said, 'Hey, Harrison, relax. I was just messing around.'

"I let him go, but I know he wasn't messing around. I knew it then, and I know it now. I knew it for sure a weak later when he was caught murdering another civilian."

"God. I'm sorry, Max."

"Yeah, it sucked." He sighed. "My point, though, is that I never reported him. I could have. The moment I saw him threatening a civilian, I could have reported him.

"But I didn't. I let him go, and for the rest of my life, I've wondered if I could have saved that civilian's life if I'd reported him. Could I have managed to get him removed from the theater so he could cope with his stress somewhere safe and healthy? Maybe, maybe not.

"But I've never beaten myself up over it. I made a mistake by not reporting him, maybe. But I made the best call available to me based on the information I had. I had to make a tough choice, and I chose wrong. You had to make a tough choice, and you were wrong. That's nothing to be ashamed of. That happens to everyone."

Jake offered his friend a small smile. "Thank you. That means a lot."

"Well, don't start feeling too happy about it. You know as well as I do that people in your line of work don't get to make those mistakes. That doesn't make you a bad person, but it still puts a damper on your future, and it still calls into question whether you're fit for this investigation."

"Well, I won't have to worry about that. Art pulled me as lead. I'm just a grunt now. He points, I shoot."

Max paused a moment. "Oh. I didn't know that."

Jake shrugged. "It's fine. I understand why he did it. To be honest, I wasn't sure if I could lead the investigation anyway. I didn't join the Secret Service to do the FBI's job."

"Well, I wouldn't get used to this. Based on what you've told me, Art is prone to having changes of heart depending on his emotional state. I would keep abreast of as much information as you can and be prepared to take over again at any given moment. I only said what I said to emphasize the position in which you've placed yourself, but it looks like you already know."

"Yes. Art and I talked last night."

"I see. Well, the second-best advice I can give you is hold your head up and keep moving forward. The goal is still to protect the President and apprehend the assholes who tried to kill him. Once the Secret Service does that, it won't matter what happened along the way. You guys will have a massive victory to hold over your head."

“Fingers crossed,” Jake agreed. “You said that’s the second-best advice. What’s the best advice?”

“Stop dating Sheila Jackson.”

Jake sighed. “I think that’s out of my hands too.”

“For now. But like your career, I think it’ll be placed in your hands again sooner rather than later. When it’s offered again, refuse. Or resign as a Secret Service agent and pursue the relationship as a private citizen. I recommend the former, but hard as it is to believe, I’ve been in love before, and I know how blind love can make someone.”

“She initiated everything,” Jake protested.

“So be the bigger person and end everything. You have to. Be honest: someone points a gun at the President and another one at Sheila. Who do you protect?”

Jake didn’t answer.

Max smiled compassionately. “That’s your answer right there. You might have to make that choice one day. If you don’t know with absolute certainty that you’d make the right one, then you need to remove whatever it is that’s clouding your judgment. Right now, that’s Sheila.”

Jake frowned and remained silent. “I know it’s a tough choice,” Max said, “but, and I say this with love, suck it up, Marine. You weren’t hired for this job because it’s easy.”

Jake nodded. “No, Master Gunny,” he said reluctantly. “I was not.”

Max laid a comforting hand on Jake’s shoulder. “I have to take over behind the counter. The dinner rush is starting. Go on home and take the night to reflect on everything. Then make the right choice.”

Jake left the bar and did exactly as Max suggested, but no matter how much time he spent reflecting, he woke the next morning still unsure what the right answer was.

CHAPTER FIFTEEN

In order to be successful as a sniper, Jake had to perfect the skill of remaining unseen. He had to be comfortable remaining motionless for long periods of time, focusing only on his target and waiting patiently for the right moment to strike. When the mission was completed, he needed to quickly and smoothly evacuate, disappearing like a phantom and leaving no trace.

In a way, being a Secret Service agent was similar. Agents were present always, but they were never talked about. They never acted in a way to make their presence known. They didn't take steps to hide themselves physically, but they were taught to blend in and remain just conspicuous enough that potential threats knew they waited to address such threats.

Jake recalled his father telling him of a suspected assassination attempt on President Reagan shortly after the botched attempt that left Reagan in the hospital. His father remembered clearly how an agent was seen tackling the President and shielding him with his body as they placed him into the limousine and evacuated the scene. That agent had risked his own life to protect the President, but no one ever talked to him. Not one journalist interviewed him about his heroism or even mentioned his actions. No one even knew his name.

And that was fine with Jake. The job wasn't about him. It was about the President, and he was perfectly content to be as anonymous as any other agent.

He didn't get to be anonymous anymore. Not at agency headquarters, at least. The moment he arrived for work the following morning, he walked straight into the arms of Internal Affairs.

The Internal Affairs agents were stone-faced individuals who introduced themselves as Agents Rodney and Kamal. They led Jake through the lobby and main office of the building without making any attempt to shield him from curious eyes. Jake would have been upset by that if he hadn't seen numerous other agents being interrogated by other Internal Affairs investigators. He saw Jess sitting in a chair across from two agents, hands folded tightly in her lap, her knuckles white with tension. He saw men he had worked with for years glare at him as he walked past. He caught a glimpse of Art sitting in his office, returning to two IA agents a look as stone-faced as the ones they gave him.

It hit him how much trouble he really was in. For the first time, he realized he actually could lose his career.

Rodney and Kamal led him to an unused office and directed him to sit behind the desk while they took the two chairs in front. Sitting in what would ordinarily be a position of power while his interrogators sat in what would ordinarily be a position of supplication lent an interesting dynamic to the conversation.

Specifically, it threw him off balance. Hell, the entire situation threw him off balance. What did they expect to learn that they didn't already know? Was this just a scare tactic designed to get him to confess to wrongdoing?

"Good morning, Special Agent Mercer," Rodney said. "As I told you earlier, my name is Special Agent Janice Rodney, and this is my partner, Special Agent Pashti Kamal. We're here to ask you some questions regarding some information that's come to light regarding your prior service history with the Marine Corps, as well as recent events that occurred during the current investigation into the assassination attempts on the President. Do you consent to having this interview recorded?"

"Do I have a choice?"

Kamal and Rodney regarded him impassively. He sighed. "Yes, I consent."

"Thank you."

Kamal set a small recording device on the desk and positioned it so the microphone faced all three of them. He pressed a button on top, and a red light blinked on above the recorder.

"Will you please confirm your name for the record?" Rodney asked.

"Senior Special Agent Jacob Mercer."

"Thank you, Mr. Mercer, and that answers my next question: your current rank. Can you please detail your current assignment?"

"To protect the President of the United States."

Rodney and Kamal shared a look. "Mr. Mercer, for the duration of this interview, you may understand it to be assumed that you share the same overarching responsibilities as every member of the Secret Service. What I'm asking is what your current specific assignment is."

Jake sighed. "To follow the orders of Director Arthur Davis."

A flash of irritation crossed Rodney's face. "Mr. Mercer, making things difficult for us will only make things difficult for you."

"I'm not trying to be difficult. That is exactly what I've been ordered to do. After the recent operation to apprehend the terrorists suspected of attempting to assassinate the President, Director Davis elected to remove me from my leadership role in this investigation and specifically instructed me to do nothing other than follow his specific directions."

"And what are those?"

"To arrive for work this morning after a mandatory forty-eight-hour leave."

Kamal and Rodney shared another look. Maybe they needed to communicate telepathically to make sure they were asking the right questions.

Rodney made a note in a small pad, then continued. "Mr. Mercer, how long were you a member of the United States Marine Corps?"

"Eight years."

"And I see from your service record that you joined the Secret Service shortly after."

"Yes."

"During the interview process, did you disclose all information related to your prior service to the interviewing agent?"

Jake's lips thinned. "No."

"You willingly withheld information from your interviewing agent?"

"The way you phrased that question suggests to me that I need a lawyer. Is it the intent of the internal affairs department to charge me with a crime?"

"Not at this time. We're simply gathering all of the information surrounding facts that have recently come to light."

Jake chuckled. "Right. Well, to answer your question, I willingly chose to provide every piece of information regarding my past that I felt was pertinent to the job of a Secret Service agent."

"And that didn't include your deployment to Afghanistan in October of 2013?"

"No."

"May I ask why?"

Jake sighed. "The resulting court-martial found me innocent of any wrongdoing. I didn't consider it necessary to revisit the event when it was already determined that I was innocent."

"Why didn't you share this information with your interviewing agent?"

"Did I not just answer that question?"

Rodney leaned back and sighed. "You could have told the interviewing agent that you were brought before a court martial and found to be innocent of any wrongdoing. Why did you not share that information?"

"Because I didn't think the interviewing agent would consider my acquittal when he made a hiring decision."

"Why?"

"I think he can give you a better answer to that question than I can."

"I'm interested in your thoughts."

Jake chuckled and shook his head. "I suppose I feared that the interviewing agent would have a different opinion on the event than the court martial did."

"Why?"

Jake lifted his hands and let them drop onto the desk. "I don't know if I have a good answer to that."

The two agents aligned their hiveminds with another glance, then looked back at Jake. Kamal took over. "Let's talk about the events of two nights ago. Can you explain your decision to apprehend three armed suspects by yourself against the recommendations of your partner?"

Jake frowned. "The intent was to reconnoiter a known meeting location of Trident and see if we could find more evidence of the organization's membership and future plans. That objective was achieved."

"And why did you then proceed to attempt an arrest without backup and with no vehicle other than your motorcycle?"

"Actually, let's go back to that," Kamal interrupted. "Why did you choose to undertake this operation without making Director Davis aware of your intentions?"

"Because I felt that time was of the essence. That proved to be the case since the terrorists left the location less than fifteen minutes after my arrival."

"How did you plan to transport the suspects without an agency van?"

"I planned to hold them at the location and wait for a Rapid Response Team to arrive to transport them."

"Did you request a Rapid Response Team?"

"Special Agent Foster did on my behalf."

"When you told Special Agent Foster of your plans, how did she react?"

"She was… concerned."

"Can you elaborate?"

Jake frowned. "At no point did Special Agent Foster act contrary to her duties as a Secret Service agent, and at no point did she violate any policy or bylaw of the Secret Service. She reacted in a manner consistent with her training and appropriate to her relationship with me and her responsibilities to the agency. That is all the elaboration you need and all the elaboration I will provide."

Kamal and Rodney shared their world-famous look, and then Rodney took over again. "How long have you been romantically involved with Sheila Jackson?"

Jake chuckled. The blunt question was a clumsy and amateurish attempt to throw him off. He had seen it coming from before the interview even started, and now that it was here, he wasn't worried about how to answer it.

"I am not romantically involved with Sheila Jackson."

"Then why did she visit you at your apartment three nights ago and then two nights ago?"

"She wished to express her concern for her father's safety and assure herself that I and my team were doing everything in our power to keep him safe."

"Why did she choose to ask you this question at your apartment and not at agency headquarters?"

"I don't feel comfortable speculating on her motives."

"How long did she spend at your apartment both nights?"

"Long enough to satisfy her concerns."

"What exactly transpired between the two of you, Mr. Mercer?"

"She expressed concern for her father's safety, and I assured her that I and my team are doing everything in our power to keep him safe."

Irritation flashed across Rodney's face once more. "Mr. Mercer, being obtuse won't help you."

"Then I'll be clear. It's none of your business how the President's daughter chooses to spend your time. I will answer for my actions, and I have. I will not share details of Miss Jackson's activities without her knowledge and approval."

The two investigators stared at Jake for a long moment. Finally, Rodney closed her notepad and put it away. "For the time being, Mr. Mercer, you may remain on active duty, though you are officially barred from taking a leadership role until this investigation is concluded. I suggest very strongly that you follow Director Davis's instructions and act only within the confines of his specific orders. Do you have any questions for me?"

"No."

"Very well."

Rodney and Kamal stood and left the office without further preamble. Jake sat at the desk and shook his head as he considered the situation.

IA was serious about dismissing him. That was clear both because of the questions asked and the manner in which the two investigators asked them.

They wouldn't proceed until after this investigation, though. Whether that was because they believed he was critical to the investigation's success or whether the agency simply didn't have the resources or energy to prosecute an internal investigation until the current crisis was over remained to be seen.

Either way, Jake had a sinking feeling that his days with the service were numbered.

Protect the President, he told himself. *That's all that matters.*

Still, it wasn't just the President's safety that remained at the front of his mind. Sheila was in danger, and right or wrong, he would do whatever he needed to make sure she was safe as well.

CHAPTER SIXTEEN

Jake leaned back and rubbed his eyes. He and Jess had worked all day to find more data on Trident or its members but had nothing to show for it.

The radio had provided them with damning evidence, but thanks to the failure of Jake's arrest attempt, that data was now useless until they captured the terrorists. The social media accounts used to comment on the President's speech had gone dark and while the NSA had managed to identify the suspects they couldn't figure out where the messages were sent from, and Jake and Jess had no idea how to follow up.

"Dammit," Jake said, standing. "I'm going to get some coffee."

"You can't leave the building, Jake," Jess reminded him. "They're watching to make sure you listen to Art."

Art had instructed Jake to assist Jess in hunting for communication channels between the Trident members. He had told Jake in no uncertain terms that he expected Jake to remain at headquarters until his duty shift was over.

Jake bristled. The President was currently addressing Congress and other agents were assigned to protect him. Jake knew nothing about the security measures in place and had no idea if it was enough to ensure the President's safety. He was effectively out of the loop.

It didn't help that Jess had been cold to him all day. He had assured her that he had made it clear that she had done nothing wrong, but she had only glared at him and reminded him that his word meant little to Internal Affairs.

She had calmed somewhat once they got started working and even made small talk with him as the investigation proceeded, but there was a distance between them that he wasn't used to. Added to everything else that was on his plate, it only soured his mood even more.

"I'm going to the break room," he assured her. "The coffee is shit there, but it has caffeine, and it still tastes better than the energy drinks they keep in the fridge. They also have stale donuts if you want sugar and don't mind sacrificing a few teeth."

She smiled slightly. “Grumble, grumble, grumble, whine, whine, whine.”

He rolled his eyes and tried not to let her see the leap of excitement he felt at knowing she wasn’t angry at him anymore. “Whatever,” he said. “I’ll get two donuts and eat both of them in front of you.”

“Big fan of eating donuts, huh?”

“I know you’re trying to set up a dirty joke, and I’m not falling for it.”

“You’re no fun when you’re angry.”

“You can be fun for both of us.”

He left the office and headed downstairs. The lighthearted moment helped a lot, but the stares her received from the other agents as he made coffee and selected two of the donuts reminded him that he was far from the most popular member of the agency right now.

Yeah, I get it. I fucked up. Everyone look at the asshole who made all of their lives so difficult.

Despite his irritation, he could understand everyone's frustration. Many of the agents questioned yesterday didn't even work closely with him. From their perspective, their careers were in jeopardy, thanks to the actions of a coworker they barely knew.

He made his way back upstairs with the coffee, but he didn’t think the infusion of caffeine would help him. His exhaustion was more mental than physical at this point.

They continued to work into the night. Art checked on them just long enough to tell Jake that he could stay as long as he wanted but that he was allowed to go nowhere other than his own apartment when he left. Jake stifled an angry retort and simply agreed to follow that instruction.

When the clock struck nine and they still hadn’t found any leads, Jess sighed and crossed her arms. She looked adorable when she was angry, but Jake wasn’t about to tell her that. Besides, he was just as upset as she was.

Then his anger gave way to shock when Jess said, “We need to tap into a satellite.”

He stared incredulously at her. “What?”

“It’s the only way we can find them. There are too many options right now, and looking through computer records and cell phone records and landline records and god-knows-what-else is going to take more time than we have.”

“How much time is more time than we have?”

“Think years, not months.”

"Oh."

"Yeah, exactly."

"So you're going to ask Art if we can talk to the NSA and get access to satellite logs?"

"The NSA won't have satellite logs. The DIA handles all of the military satellites, and the FCC handles civilian ones."

"I don't suppose you've screwed anyone at either of those agencies who might be able to help us?"

Jess glared at him, and he lifted his hands in apology. "Just asking."

"How about you be helpful instead of joking. I'm doing this for you, you know."

"Not the President?"

Jess rolled her eyes. "Do you want to keep playing stupid, or do you want to have an honest conversation about this?"

"I want to have an honest conversation. Honestly, I think this is really risky. I think that we've already landed us in a lot of trouble—"

"You've landed us in a lot of trouble."

He lifted his hands in apology again. "And I think that we need to play this aboveboard."

"Do you think Art will let us tap into a satellite?"

He hesitated a moment, then said, "No. I don't. Not without asking permission first."

"We don't have time to ask permission. The next attack could happen at any second. We need to stop this *now.*"

"I see the merit, Jess, but—"

"What's our job, Jake?"

He sighed. "To ensure the safety of the President."

"Do you think we have a better way of doing that than locating Trident and bringing them to justice?"

"Not materially, no."

"Well, then, materially, this is the best thing we can do."

He sighed. "I'm just worried that we could be earning ourselves more trouble. Like you said, it's my fault that we're in trouble now, but if you do this, then it'll be your fault."

"According to IA, not immediately reporting you to Art makes it my fault. But I'm not going to throw you under the bus. Believe me, I considered it, but it turns out I'm not capable of it. So, since I'm in for a penny, I might as well be in for a pound. Are you in, or are you going to let a little thing like the end of your career and a possible prison sentence stop you?"

He stared at her in silence for a moment. Then he said, “You’re insane, do you know that?”

“Oh, I know. It’s my favorite quality of myself.”

Jake laughed. “All right. How exactly do we go about tapping a satellite?”

She grinned. “Let me show you something.”

She sat in front of her workstation and clicked on a link in the agency’s intranet. She followed what seemed like an innocuous rabbit-trail of links until she came to a screen that read Project Puce.

He lifted an eyebrow, and she shrugged. “I didn’t choose the name.”

“So what exactly is Project Puce?”

"It's a surveillance program. For a time, the Secret Service considered taking all surveillance on threats to the President's safety in-house. The plan was to have the NSA flag communications that indicated a potential threat to the President and pass them along to us. Then, we would take over surveillance and determine appropriate responses to the threats. The program was shelved because leadership decided—probably correctly—that it didn’t make any sense to complicate a system that was already working as well as it could work.

“But the infrastructure remains.”

“And what infrastructure is that?”

“A proprietary intranet that functions more like an internet. It’s a VPN that uses existing government servers to generate code that can spy on flagged communications in the background. It’s noticeable, but only if you’re looking directly at it *and* know exactly what you’re looking for.”

“And you’re going to tag satellites?”

“Yes. Since it’s a VPN, it has access to more than enough computing power to monitor communications from multiple satellites. We can monitor all communications via those satellites, then flag anything that looks like Trident.”

“Won’t that leave us in the same position where we have to spend months sifting through information?”

“No. Satellite phones are used very rarely. Most of what we’re going to pick up is researchers in remote locations and amateur adventurers calling for rescue somewhere off the beaten path. That will make it much easier to sift through information and much easier to identify suspicious calls.”

“And much easier for us to get caught.”

"Again, only if they're looking for us and know exactly what they're looking for. Worst-case scenario, they just see something suspicious, and the moment I see them investigating, I pull us out."

Jake thought about it, but there was nothing really to think about. They were at a stalemate, and while Jake was worried about his and Jess's future, the President's safety was paramount. If the two of them lost their careers because they were doing the best they could to capture the Trident terrorists, then so be it."

He sighed. "All right. I'm in. What do you need from me?"

"I need you to go to the situation room and get me a list of serial numbers from the locked file cabinet they keep there."

Jake blinked. "What?"

"I know you heard me. Nut up, buttercup."

"Okay, really. What?"

"Nut up, buttercup. It means—"

"Yeah, I got it. I mean, you want me to break into Records?"

"No. These records won't be in records. They'll be in a filing cabinet just behind terminal I-3 in the situation room. The keyhole is just underneath the lip of the desk, but the cabinet itself will open up in front of the desk."

"You want me to break into a filing cabinet in the one part of headquarters that is staffed twenty-four-seven and get you some serial numbers?"

"Can you do it?"

"I can do it, but not without being seen."

"Then do it being seen, and if anyone asks, tell them your supervisor instructed you."

"That will get this right back to Art."

"But hopefully not until we find something. You know, Art. We give him something useful, he won't care how we got it."

"I don't know that I share your optimism there, but I'll take a chance."

"That's a bet you know will pay off."

Jake made his way to the situation room. The situation room was basically a monitor room with multiple screens connected to servers that scrolled information considered pertinent to the Secret Service's mission. Somehow, the room actually was empty. Jake wondered if Jess had arranged that somehow or if the shortage of manpower at headquarters due to heightened security had contributed.

"Hello? Who's here?"

Never mind. Jake stood and smiled at the inquirer, a security guard who frowned at him, first with authority, then, when he recognized Jake, confusion. "Special Agent Mercer? What are you doing here?"

"Hey there..." he looked at the guard's nametag. "Cameron. I'm just retrieving a file for my partner. She was a part of the project back in the day, and she needs to doublecheck something for a report she's writing."

"Now? Aren't you guys working on stopping the terrorists who attacked the President?"

Dammit, Jake hated lying. He wasn't good at it. That's why he never even considered the CIA. He decided to try playing stupid instead. To hear some people talk, he was good at that whether he tried or not.

He lifted his hands in an *I don't know* gesture. "We are, but I guess the powers that be need to clarify something in a report to Congress. The wheels of government keep on turning whether we want them to or not, am I right?"

Cameron nodded, but he didn't seem convinced. Not that Jake could blame him. The story he gave was thinner than the toilet paper in a National Park restroom. Jake would have to hope that as a security guard, Cameron would consider the business of Special Agents above his pay grade.

"Do you have clearance to be here?" Cameron asked.

Dammit.

"Clearance? Do you need special clearance? I thought any Special Agent could be here."

He waited for Cameron to talk into his radio and blow his cover. Instead, he caught a rare break.

Cameron chuckled. "Maybe. I don't know. No one tells me anything."

"I can wait until you talk to your boss if you want." Jake offered, trying to add an extra layer of believability to his stupidity.

Cameron hesitated, and Jake kicked himself mentally. It was getting easier to believe that he really was stupid.

"Nah," Cameron said. "He's in a mood today. I don't feel like bothering him. Just make sure you lock up after you're done."

He left the room, and Jake breathed a sigh of relief and retrieved the files.

Next time, Jess is the one stealing classified documents.

He made his way back to the office, files in hand.

Jess took the files and grinned at him. “Awesome. This will be good. You’ll see. Don’t worry. All we need to do is get something useful. We stop Trident, and it won’t matter how we do it.”

Jake agreed with her, but he worried that they might not stop Trident before IA caught wind of their activities and invited them to spend the next several years in a cell thinking about it.

Well, it was too late to back out now.

In for a penny, in for a pound.

CHAPTER SEVENTEEN

"Jake! Jake, wake up!"

Jake tore himself away from a very satisfying dream involving him and Sheila apologizing to each other for their argument in a very fulfilling way and groaned. He sat straight and rubbed sleep from his eyes. "Am I still at headquarters? Did I fall asleep?"

"You did, and yes, you snore very loudly," Jess said, "but that doesn't matter right now because I have something."

Jake came to full alertness immediately. "What do you have?"

"I have another location for Trident."

Jake's eyes widened. "The satellite feed gave you that?"

"No, one of our agents did."

"One of ours? Who?"

"Harris."

Jake knew Special Agent Gabriel Harris. He was a solid agent, but he was fairly limited in his abilities. He was an excellent bodyguard, but he wasn't an investigator. "How did he get this information?"

Jess stared at him for a moment. "You want to ask that and not what the information is?"

"Okay, what's the information?"

"Trident just tried to steal the President's schedule from the White House."

"Steal the President's schedule?"

"Yes. One of the Chief of Staff's employees caught a weird code on her computer. Harris commandeered the desktop and identified the signal as a data miner. He traced it to a warehouse in Arlington."

"Harris did this? Gabe Harris?"

"Yes! Jake, for God's sake, this is big! Don't tell me you suddenly have cold feet."

"You're confident this information is accurate?"

"Unless you think Harris is a liar."

"No, he's not a liar."

"Good, because Art just authorized a Rapid Response Team, and he's going to let you lead it. Well, *I'm* going to lead it, but you'll be the guy in charge on the ground. Well, on the ground outside of headquarters. You know what I mean."

"You already talked to Art about this?"

"Well, in the middle of your truly excessive snoring, you moaned Sheila's name a few times. It sounded like you were having fun, so I decided to let you sleep."

Jake felt heat climb his cheeks. "Okay. Is the team ready?"

"I imagine they will be by the time you get your ass downstairs."

"Okay, Mom. I'm going, I'm going."

"You better thank your lucky stars. I'm not your mom," Jess replied, "or you would spend the rest of your life grounded."

"Sounds good, Mom."

Jess slapped his shoulder and shooed him away. "Go!"

He laughed, giddy at the possibility of a new lead and left the room. He reached the ground floor with a grin and a spring in his step.

We have you again, asshole, he thought.

He wasn't sure who the specific asshole was in this case. Bard, he supposed. And Drew. And Jefferson. Hell, all of them. *We got all of you assholes.*

Jake didn't recognize any of the officers in the Rapid Response Team, which was probably just as well. He imagined that most people who knew him right now weren't very happy with him. He issued his instructions quickly and without preamble. Four officers would enter the building with him. The remaining officers would cover the exits and ensure that none of the Trident members escaped the building. Once the scene was secure, they would call in a team of cybercrimes experts from the FBI to crack into whatever computer they were using and gather whatever evidence they could.

Either way, this ended today.

They proceeded to the warehouse in an armored van. The RRT checked their weapons and gear with a level of professionalism that would have made the Corps proud.

"Follow my lead in there," Jake instructed them. "We all come home today, understand?"

"What about the terrorists?" one of the officers asked. "Do they go home?"

"They don't die unless they have to, but they don't go home. Not tonight or any other night for the rest of their lives."

The RRT cheered, and they reached the location, eager to put an end to the terrorist threat that had plagued their nation for two weeks now.

The building itself was in slightly better shape than the old building that Jake had discovered in Capitol Heights. On the way, Jake had checked the building records and discovered that the warehouse had belonged to Shoreline Shipping Company up until a little over a year ago. It had been purchased, not surprisingly, by EB Holdings and listed as an auxiliary storage facility.

There were no lights on in the building that were visible from the outside, but that wasn't a surprise. It was to be expected that Trident at least made a token effort at secrecy.

"When we go in, I want everyone to move cautiously. There's no need for theatrics or heroics. We have these guys, but we need to make sure we don't get ourselves hurt in the process."

The leader of the RRT, a hard-faced woman around Jake's age named Sergeant Garrett said, "I speak for everyone on this team when I tell you that we're willing to lay down our lives for the President."

"I believe you," Jake said. "That being said, I still want you all to be careful."

Garrett cracked what probably passed for a smile for her. "We'll be careful, Special Agent."

"Outstanding."

They moved quickly. The van came to a halt in front of the entrance, and they burst into the warehouse without preamble.

"Federal agents!" Jake called. "Come out with your hands up! Do not resist!"

They were greeted with silence, which wasn't terribly surprising. Jake doubted that the Trident operatives were eager to reveal themselves. He gave them another warning. "Federal agents! Come quietly, or we are authorized to fire on you!"

Still silence. Jake looked at Garrett and nodded.

The officers fanned out, moving slowly through the warehouse. The warehouse was clearly no longer used for storage, but it was still filled with shelves and pallets and empty crates that provided excellent cover for anyone who might be inside. Jake felt his heart pound and waited for any sign of the terrorists.

It wasn't until they had searched half the warehouse that it occurred to Jake that they might not find anything. Maybe Harris had been mistaken, and Trident wasn't here. Maybe Trident's VPN had somehow managed to convince the agent that they were operating here when they were really at an entirely different location.

The warehouse was nearly empty, but just as they reached the end, Jake spotted a laptop computer sitting on an empty crate. He walked toward it, but before he could open it, one of the RRT officers called. "I found a body!"

They immediately made their way to the agent, and when Jake saw the body of Gabriel Harris, his heart sank. The young agent had apparently tried to go after the terrorists himself, just like Jake had. Just like Jake, he had proven to be less than a match for multiple armed terrorists, at least two of which had combat training.

Unlike Jake, he hadn't survived.

Jake sighed and knelt by the fallen agent's body. He tapped his earpiece and said, "Hey, Jess, it's Jake."

"Hey, Jake," Jess replied.

"Yeah, we're here. We found Harris. It looks like he tried to go in on his own too."

"Oh God. How is he?"

Jake sighed. "Deceased."

Jess paused a moment. Then she said. "I see. Dammit."

"Yeah. My thoughts exactly."

"So what are you going to do?"

"I'm going to see if I can get into the computer they left behind. Maybe I can find something that will help us figure out Trident's next move. In the meantime, I'll have Sergeant Garrett call Art and tell him to have the President's schedule altered. We can assume that Trident has it now."

"That sucks."

"Yes, I know."

"I mean about Harris. That sucks."

"Yeah," he sighed. "I know."

"Okay. Well, be careful. When I've followed up with Art, I'll touch base with you. If you can't get into the computer, just bring the whole thing back to headquarters, and I'll take a look."

"I'll probably do that anyway."

"Whatever makes you happy."

Jake hung up and got to work on the computer. It was a sophisticated model, near the cutting-edge of civilian tech, but it was far too weak to be able to use the decryption software necessary to break into a private White House communication.

Someone must have leaked that information to them.

Then why the computer? Was it just a decoy, or was it used as a storage device? Or maybe it was just supposed to read information, but they needed another tool to crack the firewalls.

Either way, it was short work getting into the computer, and once he was in, it was also short work decrypting the data.

There wasn't much of it. A few articles on anarchy but nothing else of note.

Jake sighed and finally decided he would have to bring the computer to Jess to analyze it.

He returned to Harris's body and knelt down to see if Trident had left any clues that might tell him where to go next. He wasn't entirely sure what he was looking for, but when he examined Harris's watch closely, something intrigued him. He lowered his head to listen to the watch's mechanism.

Why did it sound off? How would he even know if it sounded off? Was he just being paranoid?

Art's voice sounded in his head. *Paranoia is a good quality for a Secret Service Agent. We're one of the few organizations in the world that works well with people who jump at shadows."*

He tapped his earpiece. "Jess, I'm going to bring in the computer Trident was using and Special Agent Harris's watch."

"His watch? Why his watch?"

He shook his head. "I don't know. I just have a feeling."

"Must be a hell of a feeling."

"It usually is."

"All right. Well, do whatever you have to do. I'm waiting here."

She sounded disappointed, and Jake didn't blame her. She probably felt similarly to how he felt when he failed to apprehend the three terrorists at the last hideout.

But they had evidence this time. They could…

Hold on.

He bent close to the watch again and figured out what was wrong with it. It wasn't just ticking. It was humming. Analog watches shouldn't hum.

His heart leapt. He carefully removed the watch and examined it more closely. There was a slight depression on the underside. When he pressed it, the watch face swung open, revealing the inner mechanisms of the clockwork.

And a small memory card.

Jake pumped his fist in victory. Harris's sacrifice had not been in vain. He called Jess again. "Jess, I was able to open the watch. I found a memory card buried inside. I think Harris might have caught some conversation between Trident."

"That's awesome! Way to go, Harris!"

Jake couldn't bring himself to cheer over the man's dead body, but he nodded gravely. "Send a coroner our way, and a team of CSIs. I'll make sure Harris gets a commendation for his sacrifice."

That commendation would never be seen by anyone outside the agency. Like all other Secret Service agents, Harris's heroism would go unknown outside of the service.

But Jake would know. Jake would carry his memory with him and honor the sacrifice he had made.

He saluted Harris's body, then took his jacket off and covered Harris's face. "Rest easy, Special Agent," he said softly. "You did well."

A cry from one of the RRT members pulled him from his thoughts. He looked up in alarm to see the RRT diving for cover.

Then he heard the telltale rattle of a machine gun.

CHAPTER EIGHTEEN

Jake fired through the gap in a stack of pallets and heard a cry as his shot struck home. The other Trident terrorist behind the pallets panicked and ran for the door, but a shot from Garrett dropped him.

The machine gun rattled again, and Jake hit the ground and shielded his head, wincing from the pain in his shoulder.

The machine gun was light, a 5.56 rather than the more typical 7.62mm general purpose machine guns. That meant it couldn't penetrate all the way through the wooden beam Jake hid behind, but it also meant that the operator could move easily with the weapon and fire it from the shoulder like an assault rifle.

As soon as the machine gun fire stopped, Jake sprinted for new cover. He nearly ran headfirst into the surprised machine gunner. His instincts kicked in. He drew his knife and buried it in the man's throat. The man collapsed instantly, dropping the weapon and falling to the ground.

Jake left the machine gun there and continued running. The machine gun was useful for keeping the Secret Service agents behind cover, but it was still too heavy to be of any practical use, especially in close quarters.

The carbines the RRT carried, however, were exactly what the situation called for. After the initial surprise, the RRT was able to quickly gain control of the firefight. Jake counted three terrorists dead, leaving ten more. Those ten were rapidly losing ground, however, and two more of them dropped before the others finally decided they'd had enough and ran for the door. Three more fell before the other five reached it and fled the building.

Garrett started after them, shouting for her team to follow. Jake called her on the radio.

"Capture as many alive as possible, but don't risk your life or your team's lives to do so. I'm going to get this data back to headquarters."

"Roger that. Good luck, Mercer."

The RRT chased after the terrorists, and Jake pocketed his radio and started to leave.

Then he was hit hard from behind. He cried out and fell to the ground, rolling over to his right. He felt splinters as a bullet ricocheted off of the concrete floor. His ears hummed and his vision swam. He must have been pistol-whipped to affect him like this.

He kicked ahead and felt a touch of relief when his heel connected with something solid, and he heard a cry from the terrorist he had struck. He got to his knees and threw himself at the wavy shape of the attacker. His hand closed over the terrorist's wrist, preventing him from being able to shoot Jake, and the momentum of his lunge brought the assailant to the ground.

Jake blinked, and his vision cleared further. He recognized the snarling face of the terrorist underneath him as LeShaun Mays, one of the six terrorists present at the Lincoln Memorial bombing.

He drove his head down onto LeShaun's nose, shattering it. The terrorist cried out and tried to push Jake off of him, but Jake slid over him and wrapped his neck in a chokehold. LeShaun's eyes flew open wide, and he tried to scream, but the hold was tight, and his eyes began to roll back. The hold wouldn't kill him, but it would subdue him long enough for Jake to bind him. He would question him back at headquarters.

The sound came as more of an impression than a noise. A slight pressure on the hairs of Jake's ears told him that someone was sneaking up behind him.

He was already moving when he heard the click of a hammer being cocked, and that was what probably saved his life. The bullet meant for his head instead impacted LeShaun's. The terrorist's arms and legs fluttered for a split second, then collapsed and lay still.

Jake rolled to his feet, his own handgun lifted, but the attacker kicked it from his hands. Jake lunged, once more grabbing the attacker's wrist.

Jake's shoulder spasmed, and the terrorist wrenched free.

"You bitch!" the man shouted. "I'll kill you!"

Jake recognized that voice. He rolled over his right shoulder—the one that wasn't injured—keeping a hold of the man's wrist and hooking his right arm underneath the terrorist's left armpit. As he rolled, he flipped the man over onto his back.

Gunnar Jefferson's furious eyes met Jake's, and he wrenched his gun from Jake's hand. Jake was forced to release his hold to control Gunnar's wrist, allowing Gunnar to switch his hips and drive Jake back to the ground. He landed underneath Gunnar, his thighs inside of Gunnar's.

The terrorist held tightly with his legs, pressing his hips down on Jake and controlling him in a wrestling mount position. Jake tried to shift his weight and reach for control of Gunnar's head, but Gunnar dropped a hard elbow into Jake's temple, causing his vision to swim again.

Jake grabbed onto the hand holding the gun with both of his, turning so his shoulder absorbed some of the impact from Gunnar's blows and prevented him from being knocked unconscious.

His other shoulder throbbed, and though Gunnar's blows landed on the uninjured one, Jake felt his grip weakening. He was in serious trouble. Gunnar shifted his own weight higher on Jake's body, pressuring his diaphragm and restricting his breathing. He didn't feel stronger than Jake, but with one bad arm, there was little Jake could do to counter Gunnar's attack.

Or maybe there was. After all, Jake had learned to fight in a war, not for sport. He didn't have to follow rules. He reached up and drove his thumb into Gunnar's eye. The terrorist shrieked and flinched backward. Jake jammed a finger into his other eye, and Gunnar flinched again.

Gunnar's grip on the gun loosened. Jake wrenched it free with a quick twist and aimed it at Gunnar. Gunnar grabbed it with both of his wrists and pinned Jake's hand to the ground.

To do that, he had to lift his hips off of Jake's chest. Jake exploded backward, then to the right, twisting and landing on top of Gunnar. Gunnar wrapped his legs around Jake's hips and squeezed tightly, preventing Jake from passing into a more dominant position.

That would have worked well in a refereed grappling match. In life-or-death combat, Jake was perfectly free to lift Gunnar up off of the ground and slam him hard onto the concrete floor. Gunnar cried out but hung on.

Two more slams, however, were enough to knock the terrorist out. His eyes rolled back in his head, and his hands relaxed on Jake's wrist. Jake stood and extricated himself from Gunnar, then tossed the terrorist's weapon to the side. He worked quickly, binding Gunnar's wrists and ankles behind his back while the Trident assassin was still groggy.

"Killed LeShaun…" Gunnar groaned. "Kill you…"

"Yeah, I know," Jake said, "Life's a bitch, ain't it?"

He hefted Gunnar over his shoulder. Gunnar struggled, but Jake had tied his bonds tightly and he could do no more than wriggle slightly as Jake carried him to the van. Halfway there, the terrorist turned and tried to bite Jake's ear. Jake flinched away, then landed a punch into Gunnar's groin. Gunnar gasped and moaned, his face turning red.

"Behave yourself, and I won't have to do that again," Jake said. "You're under arrest. You have the right to remain silent. You have the right to an attorney, and… that's all I can remember. Not that it matters. You're a terrorist who's tried at least once to kill the President, so I can't imagine anyone's going to be very worried about your rights."

"Fuck you."

"That is definitely not one of your rights."

Jake reached the van and secured Gunnar in the back. He radioed Garrett. "I got one of them. Where are you?"

"We're on our way back. The terrorists had a getaway vehicle, and they were able to elude us. We were going to give chase once we reached the van. Should we still plan on that?"

"Negative. The one we got is one of the men present at the Lincoln Memorial bombing and a senior member of Trident. He'll give us all of the information we need."

"Outstanding."

Garrett arrived a moment later. Other than a graze on one of the RRT member's shoulders, the Secret Service officers were unharmed.

Garrett offered a sharklike grin to their prisoner. "Well, aren't you a handsome boy? I'm gonna sit right next to you and keep you some company on the way back to headquarters."

Gunnar paled a little, and Jake suppressed a smile as Garrett sat next to him and wrapped her arm around his shoulders. "Hey, baby," she said, making her voice a lilt. "You want to talk to me? I'm *much* nicer than Jake there. Maybe if you answer my questions, I can keep being nice to you."

Gunnar swallowed nervously, and the other RRT members laughed.

"I think he likes you, Sarge," one of them said.

"Of course he likes me," Garrett replied, "I'm a good girl."

The RRT leader continued to tease Gunnar as Jake drove them back to headquarters. Gunnar recognized the banter as her way of controlling her seething anger and wisely kept his mouth shut. When they reached headquarters, Garrett slapped Gunnar, just softly enough that she could claim playfulness but hard enough that Gunnar knew she definitely wasn't playing.

"See you around, pretty boy." She looked at Jake. "Let me know if you need help making him talk." She offered him another sharklike grin. "I can be *very* persuasive."

Jake offered Gunnar an equally hard grin. “I’ll let you know. Maybe he’ll wise up and tell us what we need to know without making things difficult.”

“Stranger things have happened, I suppose.”

Jake carried Gunnar into the building. The other agents stared wide-eyed as he carried his bound package to the holding cells in the basement. He left Gunnar there to stew for a while, then headed up to Jess’s office to turn over the thumb drive he had recovered.

Jess greeted him with a smile that turned instantly into a look of concern. “Jesus, what happened to you?”

“I got into a fight with Mike Tyson. I thought the whole badass heavyweight boxer thing was a hoax. Guess I was wrong.”

Jess rolled her eyes. “Okay, I’ll take this”—she grabbed the thumb drive—“You get your ass to the infirmary. Now, or I’ll tell Art you helped me hack into a satellite.”

“There’s no need to threaten me,” he said, “I’ll go take care of myself.”

“The only way to make you listen is to threaten you. God, your poor mother must have gone crazy raising you.”

“Believe me, Jess. I would *never* disobey my mother.”

“Sure you wouldn't. You're such a straight-laced kid."

“I might not be straightlaced, but I’m not suicidal.”

“Infirmary!” she pointed at the door. “Now!”

“All right. Chill out. Don’t get your panties in a bunch.”

“I’ll give you another reason to go to the infirmary if you’re still here by the end of this sentence.”

Jake, fortunately, was just outside the doorway at the end of that sentence and didn’t need to find out exactly what Jess planned to do to him.

The nurse at the infirmary looked him up and down and sighed. She shook her head and muttered something under her breath about overgrown boys.

Jake took the scolding in stride and allowed the nurse to perform first aid on his many cuts and bruises. As the elation of his capture receded, he began to feel the pain in his body from the firefight and the encounter with LeShaun and Gunnar.

He would go talk to Gunnar as soon as he was released. They needed the data from the thumb drive, and they needed Gunnar to talk ASAP.

He reached for his phone to call the warden and tell him to have Gunnar prepped for interrogation, but his phone buzzed before he could dial the number.

It was another text from a private number. This one read *Tick, tock, tick, tock* followed by an hourglass emoji.

Jake felt a chill creep up his spine. The message the anonymous party sent him was clear.

Time was running out.

CHAPTER NINETEEN

Jake endured the nurse's ministrations but ignored her command that he spend the rest of the day resting. It was clear that he didn't have time to rest. Whatever Trident had planned, they intended to act on it soon.

He headed back to Jess's office, and she glanced up at his bandaged face and said, "Better. I still think you should rest before you throw yourself into the meat grinder again."

"Can't rest," he replied.

He showed her the message on his phone, and her eyes widened. "I need you to figure out who sent this message. If it's a burner phone, see if you can get the serial number so we can track when it was sold and to who."

"I'll look into it," she said, "In the meantime, how do I reach you since I'll have your phone?"

"I'll have Equipment get me a burner and text you from it."

"How do I know it's you?"

"I'll send you a picture of my naked body. You can identify me by the—"

"All right," she said, rolling her eyes. "No time to rest but time to joke. Got it."

"Always. Anything from the thumb drive yet?"

She shook her head. "No, it's heavily encrypted, just like the radio. I'll get into it, but it's going to take at least the rest of the day. Hopefully longer, but I'm being realistic."

"Just do what you can."

"That's got to be the silliest phrase of encouragement ever invented."

"You're the best, Jess."

He started for the door, and she called, "Hey, where are you going?"

"To talk to Gunnar."

He left the office, but he didn't get to talk to Gunnar. He made it about five yards past the door when he ran right into Special Agents Rodney and Kamal.

"I can't talk now, guys," he said, "I'm in the middle of a time-sensitive investigation."

"We assigned another agent to talk to your prisoner," Rodney informed him.

"You *what?*" Jake thundered. "What gave you the right to do that?"

The two IA agents retained the infuriating calm for which the department was known. "As of three minutes ago, this is an official Internal Affairs investigation."

"It wasn't official before?"

"Allow me to clarify," Kamal said. "As of three minutes ago, you are being officially investigated for unlawfully withholding information pertinent to your application to the Secret Service and for engaging in an illicit relationship with a high-value client of the agency."

Jake blinked. "What does that mean?"

"It means you are only allowed to work at the discretion of the Internal Affairs department, and right now, you are not allowed to work."

Jake stared at the two of them. He nearly exploded with anger, but he calmed himself with a deep breath. "Agents, I understand that you have to do your jobs, but this is not the time to stand in my way. The President of the United States is under threat of imminent attack, and I am in the middle of a very sensitive part of the investigation that could very well prevent that attack."

"We have confidence that your fellow agents and officers will perform just as well without you as with you."

Jake struggled mightily to keep an even tone. "Yes, but I've been working this case for the past two weeks."

"So has your partner, Special Agent Foster. As part of the deal with Director Davis, the investigation against her will be dropped. She will assume secondary leadership of the investigation under Director Davis's leadership."

"She and I work better together. If we—wait, a deal?"

"Yes."

"What deal? You made a deal with Art to let Jess work but investigate me?"

"Yes. We understand that there is a highly sensitive anti-terrorist operation going on at the moment. However, we cannot in good conscience overlook the violations you have committed. We asked the Deputy Director for permission to remove you from the field. He stated that he was willing to remove you as long as your partner was able to continue working."

Jake didn't reply. His mind worked overtime trying to process what he had just heard.

Art had thrown him to the wolves. Why? Over a botched op from ten years ago when he wasn't even a member of the agency? Less than a week ago, he had told Jake how much he respected him. He had even told him that he saw something special in him, something that made him one of the finest agents he'd ever served with.

Now, he was allowing Jake to be removed from a case that was critically important to the President's safety and the safety of the nation as a whole.

"If you'll please come with us, Special Agent."

Jake met Rodney's eyes and said coldly, "If the President dies because I wasn't there to stop it, that will be your fault."

"No," Rodney replied just as coldly. "It will be yours."

Jake didn't protest further as the two agents led him away. He was keenly aware of the stares directed his way and the judgment on many of his fellow agents' faces.

Art had thrown him to the wolves. He had bargained for Jess's safety by sacrificing Jake's future.

Jake was happy that Jess was okay. If anyone was going to suffer for his actions, it should be him. He just wished that suffering could take place after he made sure that the President was safe.

The IA agents led him into an office similar to the last one they had interrogated him in. They sat across from him, and Rodney leaned forward, clasping her hands on her thighs.

"I'll cut right to the chase, Mr. Mercer. The agency knows that you illegally hacked into a communications satellite and used data from that satellite to inform your recent operation."

"Does the agency know that we were also able to capture a thumb drive containing valuable data along with one of the principal actors in the Lincoln Memorial bombing?"

"We do, which is why you're not in handcuffs."

"But it's also why I'm not allowed to work the case."

"Yes."

"So my successful action which resulted in significant progress and the apprehension of a known terrorist is the reason why I can't continue to make progress and apprehend known terrorists."

"Do you not trust your team to handle this case without you?"

Jake sighed. "I'm not going to let you twist my words. I have the utmost faith in my team. I also feel that I am critical to the investigation. Believing that removing me from the case is the wrong decision is a reflection of my lack of faith in *your* judgment and abilities, not those of my partner."

Rodney sighed. "May I be frank with you?"

"Have you been dishonest before now?"

Jake wasn't proud of the joy he felt seeing irritation cross Rodney's face, but he didn't feel particularly bad about it either.

"Mr. Mercer, the agency cannot afford the media circus that is currently surrounding you, and neither can this administration."

"Does the order to remove me from this case come from the President."

Rodney's scowl deepened. "The President has better things to do than bother himself with the Secret Service's internal matters."

"He does," Jake agreed, "which is why I imagine he'll be pissed when he has to call you and Director David personally to have me reinstated onto his personal security detail and placed in charge of the Trident investigation once more. I have a feeling that the two of you might be looking at a reassignment in the near future."

Kamal laughed. "Really? Come on, Mercer. You expect us to believe that you're going to call the President on us?"

"No. I imagine it'll be very shocking to you when the President contacts the Secret Service and reverses your decision to sideline me."

Kamal's smile faded. He and Rodney shared a glance. Rodney sighed and rubbed her eyes. In a more conversational tone than before, she said, "Jake… can I call you Jake?"

"No."

She rolled her eyes. "Mr. Mercer. The agency is being scrutinized very heavily right now. It looks very bad that we hired a man with a checkered military pas, and—"

"My military past is not checkered, Special Agent Rodney. I was honorably discharged after eight years of commendable service. I received a silver star, a bronze star, and two purple hearts. I don't like throwing that around, but my past was decorated, not checkered. The media—and the agency—is choosing to conflate and misinterpret an isolated incident. It will be too bad if the President dies as a result of your negligence, especially when I tell everyone every single reason it happened and who exactly, by name and physical description, is to blame."

Rodney frowned. "Are you threatening us?"

"Yes. Absolutely. If you fuck with my ability to protect the President, I will make it my mission in life to ruin you. You want to play hardball with me, I'll play hardball with you. But no matter what happens, I *will* protect the President. You can be absolutely certain of that."

He stood before Rodney could reply. "I'm going to continue to work on the Trident case. If I end up in trouble as a result, I'll know that my next call needs to be to the President."

He left the two IA agents to consider his words and stormed directly to Art's office. Art was in a meeting with the leads of the RRT teams, except for Garrett, who was still debriefing her team. He looked up and frowned when he saw Jake.

"Hey, Art," Jake said, "Take five. You and I need to talk."

Art's scowl deepened. "Special Agent Mercer, I am in a closed-door meeting with—"

"Meeting's over. We're now going to talk about why you threw me under the bus for political reasons."

Art sighed and rubbed his eyes. "Take five, guys."

The RRT leads left the room. Some glared at Jake on the way out, while others nodded with approval. Garrett had probably already started spreading the word about Jake's actions in the recent firefight.

When the last RRT lead left the office, Art said, "Okay. Let's talk, Jake. Before you tell me what a piece of shit I am, I want you to think about what would have happened if your little stunt with the satellite *didn't* work. What if you didn't catch that thumb drive or apprehend a terrorist?

"I'll tell you what would happen. The FCC would have my fucking head. And yours. And the entire Secret Service. The headline of every single news agency in the country would be GOVERNMENT SPIES ON PRIVATE CITIZENS. You remember when that was the big news years ago, right? When that NSA guy leaked a ton of private information to the news media, and the government was nearly crucified? Hell, a lot of people were crucified. We swung from one side of the political spectrum as a nation to the polar opposite side. *You* would have been responsible for that."

"I don't give a fuck about politics, sir."

"I do. I have to. *We* have to."

Jake frowned. "The Secret Service is responsible for protecting the President of the United States regardless of politics."

"And Santa Claus is real. And if you wish real hard, you'll go to Neverland and fly around with Tinkerbell."

Jake glared at Art. "Sir, you know I'm the best choice to run this mission. You know I'm the one the President would want."

“Since when did the President become a security expert? Jake, you—”

His phone rang. Whoever was calling must have been important, because Art frowned and answered. “Davis. Hello, sir. Yes. No, I… Yes, sir. Yes, sir.”

He hung up and pressed his palms to his temples. When he looked at Jake again, Jake saw something disturbingly close to hate. “All right, Jake,” he said in a deadly calm voice. “You win. You’re back on the case. And IA is suspending their investigation into your fitness to be an agent. Congratulations. The sun shines on you. Now get the fuck out of my office.”

Jake chose not to rub Art’s face in it. He wasn’t sure who had called Art. If the President had intervened on his behalf, he heard about the situation from someone other than Jake.

Either way, Jake was grateful. He would almost certainly be searching the classifieds for jobs once this mission was over, but for now, he could keep the President—and Sheila—safe.

CHAPTER TWENTY

News went from good to bad very quickly. Jake opened the door to Jess's office, and his partner collided with him, crying out in shock. He steadied her, and when he saw the wide-eyed look of panic on her face, he frowned. "What now?"

"I decoded the thumb drive," she said, "It contains detailed blueprints of the entire D.C. power grid and outlines plans to strike critical areas and cause a cascade failure of the entire system."

"Trident's trying to turn the city dark?"

"Dark and isolated. The government agencies have battery backup for critical systems that can last maybe one day before we start deciding between internet or medical equipment."

Jake sighed and ran his hands through his head. "Well, shit. I guess we know what we're doing for the rest of the day."

"That's what I was going to ask you. I'm worried that Trident might be trying to thin us out."

"He's not going to thin the Secret Service out. We're going to reach out to other agencies and use them to guard the power infrastructure. Our people will remain focused on protecting the President and apprehending the terrorists."

"Yes, but we can't be everywhere, Jake. There aren't very many of us."

"We don't need to be everywhere. We only need to protect the President and his family."

"That's not true, though," she retorted, fear making her irritable. "We're also responsible for the Vice President and the Cabinet members and their families. And if law enforcement is wrapped up protecting the power grid, that makes it much easier for Trident to move around. And…"

She bit her lip and looked away. The unconscious movement reminded Jake uncomfortably of Sheila.

"I'm worried that Trident's goal might not be assassinating the President."

Jake frowned. "Why would that not be their goal? They've already tried to assassinate him, and they've stolen his schedule."

"They know that his schedule will change entirely now that we know they have access to it. They also tried to assassinate the Vice President. I just feel like their goals are larger than a simple assassination, and attacking the power grid supports the hypothesis that they have bigger things planned."

"What could be bigger than assassinating the President?"

"I don't know. That's why I'm worried."

Jake took a breath and placed his hands on Jess's shoulders. "Jess, I need you to be strong for me. I know this is terrifying. Believe me. I've been in combat, and this is far more stressful than anything I've ever done in the Corps." *Most things, anyway.* "We can handle this. Trident isn't as strong or powerful as they seem. They're terrorists. Terrorists are very good at being terrifying, but when you peel the façade back, they're small-time. We're the Secret Service. We haven't lost a President in sixty years, and we won't lose this one just because Eli Bard is the one fighting us. You're right. Bard's goals may go beyond simple assassination. That won't change anything, though. We're going to do what we can do, and we're not going to worry about what we can't do. It just so happens that what we can do is ensure that the President and the rest of the Executive branch is safe. No matter what.

"So… get me the head of the Washington Police Department on the phone and tell him that we have a strong reason to suspect an assault on the Washington, D.C. power grid, and we need officers assigned to protect the grid around the clock until we determine the exact nature of the threat."

Jess nodded. She took a deep breath and smiled mischievously up at him. "Ooh, Jake. Your hands are so strong."

He took his hands off of her shoulders and rolled his eyes. "Ha ha. Get on the horn. And send the map of the power grid that you downloaded from the thumb drive to my phone. I'm going to start coordinating a defensive plan."

"You got it, honey."

He rolled his eyes again, but he was smiling when he left the office.

His smile didn't last long. As he drove to the headquarters of the Washington D.C. Department of Water and Power, the enormity of the threat struck him.

The Washington power grid was massive. It didn't just serve the residents of D.C., but the residents of the fifth-largest metropolitan area in the nation. There were nearly seven million people in the metro, not to mention the headquarters of nearly every major government agency in the United States. The Pentagon, the FBI, the NSA, the CIA, the

Capitol, the White House, Homeland Security—cutting off power to that metro would result in a catastrophe the likes of which hadn't been seen since 9/11.

The more practical issue was finding the resources to protect that power grid. D.C. wasn't the largest metro by land area, but even the relatively compact D.C.-Arlington-Capitol Heights CSA was vast when compared to the number of law enforcement officers available to watch the many power stations and transformer arrays that served the area.

Jess might be right. Trident might be trying to thin them out. If so, they had picked an outstanding way to do it. They couldn't just ignore a threat to the power grid. If this *was* Trident's plan, then he could throw the entire nation into turmoil.

An even more uncomfortable thought came to Jake's mind. What if Trident was planning to do both? Or either? If they were spread too thin to protect the President and his cabinet, then Bard could finally succeed in assassinating one of the senior executives. If they were able to protect the executives but they couldn't adequately watch the power grid, then he could cripple critical infrastructure and leave Washington floundering.

That was the other side of being a terrorist organization. Trident might not be large, and they might not have a wealth of resources available to them, but they were fast and mobile and stealthy. In a word, they were flexible. If plan A didn't work, they had plans B through Q ready to go on a moment's notice.

And they knew it.

Jake's thoughts were dark when he reached DWP headquarters, but he kept his misgivings buried. They needed to see him confident right now, not panicked.

Washington Police was already there, and Jake walked with the captain on scene to the conference room where they would meet with DWP leaders to discuss their defense strategy.

"How imminent is this attack?" the captain asked Jake.

"We should assume any moment," Jake replied.

The captain nodded, but he didn't seem satisfied. "And you're sure this isn't a hoax?"

"I'm sure that if it's not a hoax, the nation will be in grave trouble."

The captain nodded. "Fair enough."

They reached the conference room, and a heavyset man with a short gray beard introduced himself as the director and asked, "So… how bad is it?"

“At the moment, we’re not sure if there’s any substance to the threat,” Jake said, speaking diplomatically. “But we’re taking all precautions anyway, just in case.”

“What kind of interruptions should we plan on?” the director asked.

Jake felt a flash of irritation. They were warning him about a possible terrorist attack on his department, and he was worried about sending brownout notices.

He reminded himself that civilians weren’t used to dealing with the kind of threat they faced now. It was easy for Jake to think always of the potential consequences of inaction. He was trained to take every threat seriously, no matter how outlandish. Lately, he had been made very aware of just how real some of these outlandish threats could be.

But civilians couldn’t know. To the director, this was just alarmism, jumping at shadows and impacting real, practical necessities as a result.

Jake decided to be blunt. “I don’t have the expertise to answer that question. You and Captain Delaney will determine the specifics of the protection offered. I’m here to ensure that the protection is enough to keep you safe from terrorist attack. If I find it lacking, I will obtain more resources to fill in whatever gaps the Washington Police Department can’t fill.

“In general, though, sir, the answer is that you can expect as many service interruptions as are necessary to ensure that the power remains on for critical infrastructure and government.”

The director sighed. He was clearly irritated with the situation, but he at least didn’t protest further. “All right. What do you need from me?”

"I need a list and a map of all critical pieces of your infrastructure, with the most critical listed at the top. Think doomsday scenario. What absolutely needs to remain intact to provide power to the government? After that, what really should remain intact to make your life easier, but you could live without it if you had to? Then what could be sacrificed but hopefully doesn't have to be, and finally, what is extraneous or ancillary and you could lose it without risk to the government's power supply. At the very bottom of that list is civilian power."

The director didn’t say anything out loud, but Jake could see by the look on his face that he had opinions about the fact that the civilians took second fiddle here.

Jake sighed. "Look, I get it. I hate leaving regular citizens high and dry, too, but the number one priority here is keeping the President safe. I'm sorry. That's just the way it is."

The director sighed. "Yeah. I know. Hold on, I'll get you what you need."

Once Jake had the information he needed, he left Captain Delaney behind with the director to coordinate WPD protection while Jake drove to the most critical locations on the list and spoke with leadership at each location to ensure their security needs were met. As he drove, he called the tier two locations and worked out the basics over the phone. The more places he could close off to Trident access, the greater likelihood they had at success.

Jake returned to Secret Service headquarters late that evening, exhausted. Jess greeted him with equal exhaustion, but the dark circles under her eyes worried him far less than the tension in her shoulders.

"I can see by your face that you have some bad news," he said. "Is this the kind of bad news I should get coffee for?"

She nodded. "I'm afraid so. Looks like another long night for us."

Jake sighed. "I'm just going to buy a cot and sleep in the office. All right. I'm going to get us some coffee, then we'll work through the latest bit of bad news."

"Can you make mine black?"

Jake lifted an eyebrow. "That bad, huh?"

"It's bad."

"In that case, tell me now, and I'll get coffee after."

She showed him a message she had decoded from the thumb drive. His face fell when he read it.

The message was from Drew to Bard. He was letting Bard know that the strike team would be ready to enter the White House as soon as the power went out.

Well, he was sure about one thing. Their end goal was indeed to kill the President.

And as much as Jake hated to admit it, this looked like their best plan so far.

CHAPTER TWENTY ONE

Jake wasn't sure if it was correct to say that things were going from bad to worse. They were already pretty bad to begin with. Bad to still bad?

"Oh, shit," Jess said.

If I had a dollar... Jake thought glumly. "What is it?"

She turned her monitor so he could see.

Oh, it was worse. It was *much* worse.

"The President didn't cancel that dinner?"

"You're closer to him than I am. Did he say he was canceling the dinner?"

"We're not *that* close. I met him when he was a Congressman, and we've stayed in contact, but I'm not his best friend or anything like that. He wouldn't tell me if he was canceling the dinner unless it impacted my job. Actually, he *would* have told me if he was canceling the dinner if my job was still to remain glued to his side at all times. Since I'm the agency's first cop, he probably hasn't felt a need to keep me in the loop."

"Well, see if you can convince him to reschedule the dinner. The best way to keep him safe is if he's not there when Trident strikes."

Jake doubted that the answer to his problems would be that simple.

And he was right.

"No."

"No? Bry—Mr. President, this is a very real threat."

"I am surrounded by very real threats, Jake, not just to my person, but to the entire country and the majority of the rest of the world with it. My job is to address threats twenty-four-seven-three-sixty-five until the next poor fool swears an oath and sits in the big chair. I am *not* going to be cowed. I am *not* going to hide. I am *not* going to tell an already fearful nation that their leader is flinching back every time some two-bit terrorist says he's going to kill me. This state dinner *will* happen. We *will* send a message to Trident, this nation, and the world that we are strong and resolute."

"With all due respect, Mr. President—"

"That phrase is never followed by due respect," the President interrupted. "So I'll stop you there and tell you that argument is pointless. You're going to point out that my assassination will make all of my fears come to light. So make sure I'm not assassinated. You're going to say that's easier to do when I put my safety first. I'm going to remind you that my safety is nothing compared to the integrity of our government. You're going to chafe and whine about the fact that you have to acknowledge real threats while I'm downplaying them and making them look small. Guess what? I am downplaying them and making them look small. It's *your* job to crush them and make them nonexistent. I can spend the next five hours lecturing you and telling you exactly why my response is the correct one, but I'm not going to, because you don't need to know that. You just need to do your job." His voice softened, and he said, "This is the risk I chose to take when I announced my candidacy, Jake. I know you'll do everything in your power to protect me. I have faith you'll succeed, even if you don't. For all your concern, Jake, you have yet to let me down. Remember that."

He hung up, and Jake sat back in his chair and let the conversation settle in his mind. He hadn't expected Bryan to listen to him, but it bothered the hell out of him that he wouldn't. He was playing right into Trident's hands.

He felt a flash of anger at Bard. The man was using his knowledge as a former Secret Service agent to engineer circumstances that forced the President and the Secret Service to play right into his hands. He was playing a chess match, and he was winning.

Incredibly, though, the strongest feeling he walked away with was confidence. Bryan's words to him at the end of the call actually cut through Jake's fear and self-doubt and made him believe in himself again.

He chuckled. Bryan was irritating as hell sometimes, but it was easy to see why he had become President.

He returned to Jess and said, "Okay. So the dinner's on, as I expected. Bryan gave me the whole spiel about standing defiantly in the face of terror, yadda yadda, purple mountain's majesty."

Jess chuckled and said, "Wow. So patriotic."

"Oh, whatever. He's not the one who has to defend him and the entire damned cabinet from a known, planned terrorist attack. So I'll make fun of him all I want. Behind his back, of course."

"Of course."

"So this is what we need to do. We need to play to our strengths. What do we have that Trident doesn't have?"

"Numbers and resources?"

"Numbers and resources. We're going to call DARPA and get the most advanced surveillance equipment they make. We're going to place it all over the White House and all up and down Pennsylvania Avenue. We're going to put Secret Service agents everywhere. Plainclothes agents in the White House and in every business on Pennsylvania Avenue. Officers surrounded the building. Special Agents assigned to every guest with RRTs on standby at all four corners of the White House and one in the building. If Trident is a missile, we're going to be a thirty-foot thick nuclear bunker."

"I like it. Very 'Murica."

"Now who's being unpatriotic?"

"I said I like it! I didn't roll my eyes and make fun of the President."

"Yeah, well, you don't know him like I do."

The next three days were among the most exhausting of Jake's career. They weren't particularly exhausting physically, but the mental exercise of planning, organizing and arranging the most involved security plan in the service's history taxed Jake to his limit. Jess had a contact at DARPA—"Not *that* kind of contact," she was quick to point out—who gave them crates of camera and monitoring equipment that could track electromagnetic emissions all the way from infrared to microwave radio. Jake had Jess lead the installation of that equipment. She would monitor the situation from Secret Service headquarters while Jake managed the field teams from the White House.

Art was stony in Jake's interactions with him, but to his credit, he kept the focus on the task at hand and not on the ongoing snafu with internal affairs. When Jake thought about it, the rift in his working relationship with Art hurt. He had considered the man a friend, and to know that Art despised him as much as he did now was incredibly painful.

At the same time, he knew that a lot of it had to do with the stress of their current situation. Once Trident was dealt with, Jake was confident that a lot of the animosity between them could be repaired. In the meantime, they had a job to do, and angry as he was, Art was willing to do it.

At Jake's request, Garrett would oversee the RRTs. One team would stage in the Eisenhower building. Another would stand by in the Treasury Building. A third team would wait in Lafayette Square, and a fourth in the Ellipse just south of the South Lawn.

The fifth team would position themselves in the hidden room just behind the dining room where the state dinner would take place. In the event of an assault, the team would join the Special Agents in the dining room and escort the VIPs to the underground tunnel and from there to the various outposts for extraction.

The outposts themselves, and the tunnels that linked them, were watched by hundreds of officers. Trident would have no way in.

Jake told himself that at least a thousand times as he walked the perimeter and ensured everything was in place. He met with team leaders and encouraged them to stay vigilant. Occasionally, he traded banter with the leaders, talking about how foolish Trident would be to make a move tonight and how much fun they'd have taking the terrorists out tonight if they were that foolish. With other, more somber team leads, he reviewed protocols and contingency plans and assured them that no angle had been left unexplored in their preparations for the dinner.

The VIP escorts got a speech of their own. Jake made it clear that they were to maintain a professional calm at all times. As far as the VIPs were to see, this was just a normal day.

Of course, they'd have to be blind not to notice the massive uptick in security. Still, appearances counted for everything in Washington, even for those to whom appearances were supposed to be irrelevant.

Days like this, Jake missed the Marine Corps.

He tapped his earpiece and said, "Ground one to Air one. How are we looking up there?"

"We're good," Capitol Police Lieutenant Harry Peterson replied. "Airborne in five minutes. Andrews just confirmed they have a flight of F-35s ready to provide top cover if Trident tries any of that drone shit again."

"F-35s? Wow. Glad to see the Air Force is putting that budget increase to good use."

"Between you and me, I think they're all praying that Trident tries something. It would be nice to remind those assholes why you don't fuck with us."

Jake wasn't sure he felt the same way. On one hand, it *would* feel good to put an end to Trident once and for all, and if they came out in force tonight, it was possible that they could do just that.

On the other hand, if they didn't try anything, then no one would get hurt.

Jake went through the patrol patterns for the four helicopters Capitol Police would use to monitor the airspace and the four they would use to monitor the ground. This was going to be a very expensive security response, but as long as it was effective, Jake didn't give a damn how much it cost.

His final phone call was to the President. "All right, sir. We've got everything locked up tight. I won't waste time asking you to keep this brief, but I'll tell you that we're prepared for any threat that will arise."

"I know you well enough to know that you're asking me to keep this brief. The best I can do is promise that it will be brief for a state dinner."

Jake chuckled in spite of his anxiety. "I'll let everyone know to settle in."

"Sounds good. Hey, chin up, will you, Jake? You guys are the best in the business. You have nothing to worry about."

"It's not myself I'm worried about, sir. It's you and your family."

"Well, Carrie and Sheila are in the bunker, so unless Trident stole the nuclear launch codes somehow, they'll be okay. As far as me, well, like I said, it's the risks of the job. I'm not hiding anymore."

"I know, sir. Good luck."

"I won't need it. I have you."

Jake sighed when the President hung up. "God, I hope that's enough."

With the preparations complete, Jake returned to the White House. He would monitor everything from a situation room similar to Jess's setup at Secret Service headquarters and direct resources as necessary.

The guests arrived one by one. The Vice President was first, and judging by her pissed-off look, Jake surmised she was having a good day.

After her, the Secretary of State arrived, followed by the Secretaries of Homeland Security and Health and Human Services. The Cabinet arrived in groups of two and three after that, and the last to arrive, ten minutes late in true general officer hypocrisy, was the Secretary of Defense.

"Be advised," Jake said, "All eggs are in the basket."

His team leaders acknowledged one by one, and Jake settled in to prepare for the long and very stressful evening.

"Okay, Bard. Your move."

CHAPTER TWENTY TWO

The hors d'oeuvres and salad courses went by without incident. When the appetizers were served and consumed without any sign of trouble, Jake began to feel himself relax slightly. When the main course was served and well on its way to completion, he released a breath he hadn't realized he'd been holding.

They weren't out of the woods yet. Once the main course was over, the President would get to the business portion of the meeting. Ostensibly, these state dinners were supposed to be business-free, but Bryan wasn't the sort of President to endorse unnecessary free time on the taxpayer's dime. The people were funding this meeting, so the people attending it would damn well get some work done.

The length of the meal would depend entirely on how much argument people would want to have, and that would depend entirely on what policies Bryan wanted to discuss and how bullish he intended to be about them. Unfortunately, while Bryan was well-known for his softspokenness when addressing the public, he was equally well-known in Washington for being stubborn as a mule when addressing policymakers.

Jake would just have to hope that he could keep the current situation in mind and keep the infighting to a minimum today.

Either way, they were over the hump. The business would conclude, and then there would be dessert and coffee. More than a few of the attendees would drink too much and have to be discreetly escorted out lest the news media catch wind of any poor behavior. Others would want to shoot the breeze long past the time they wore out their welcome and have to be gently coaxed away by members of the White House staff.

But things were going well. The power was still on. There had been no sign of Trident anywhere, and Jake and his resources were doing everything they needed to keep things safe.

So, of course, the bottom had to fall out at some point.

It started when the last of the main course was cleared away. Jess called him to report suspicious activity on the corner of Constitution and 12th Street, in the vicinity of the Smithsonian.

"What kind of suspicious activity?"

"SUVs with dark tinted windows. Looks like two of them proceeding toward the barrier at fifteenth street."

"Special Agent Mercer, this is Special Agent Marquess."

"Go ahead, Marquess."

"I'm seeing the same thing on the other side of the Ellipse. Two SUVs proceeding toward the barrier. If they don't turn left at 18th Street, then they're heading here."

"Stop them. All four of them. Shoot them if you have to, but do *not* let them past the barrier. Air One, do you copy?"

"I copy, eyes on the trucks. They are… turning. Two down 14th and two down 18th."

"Follow them. Light them up while you do to let them know you see them. Ground five, ground six, you two read me?" The two team leaders acknowledged, and he said, "Watch those vehicles. They do anything suspicious at all, I want them turned into charcoal. Got it?"

"Got it. Barbecued terrorists, coming right up."

"I appreciate the sentiment, five, but let's save the rest of the banter for after the dinner."

"Understood, sir."

No sooner had Jake dealt with that threat than his personal cell phone buzzed. Sheila.

His heart thumped, and when he answered, she had little in the way of encouragement to offer. "Jake? Someone just texted me, 'Enjoy the end.'"

"Who?"

"I don't know. Another burner phone."

She was keeping herself under control, but the tension in her voice belied her fear. Jake forced his own panic away and said, "Have you seen or heard anything suspicious in the bunker?"

"No, everything seems fine here."

"Okay. I'm going to hang up and call the team lead in charge of your safety. You're getting out of there. We're taking you to Delta."

Aside from Alpha, Outpost Delta was the most secure of the underground holding facilities that protected the President and his family in case of a catastrophic emergency. He would have chosen Alpha, but it was too close to the White House.

"Okay. You stay safe too, Jake."

Jake didn't imagine there would ever be a chance for the two of them to connect in anything other than a professional way again, but hearing her express concern for him filled him with longing. He pushed it away and made himself focus on the task at hand.

He tapped his earpiece and said, "Okay, everyone, we're going to Code Yellow. We have suspicious vehicles near the White House and threatening messages sent to the President's daughter. Quiver One, take the President's family to Outpost Delta and confirm when you arrive."

"Will do."

"Air One, tighten your pattern and scan for everything. Call Dulles and George Washington and make sure all commercial flights are diverted around the city. Might as well call Andrews and tell them to scramble the jets. They can leave them on the runway for now, but they need to be ready to take off the moment I say."

"Understood."

"White House One, I want all nonessential personnel evacuated ASAP. The only people who stay are the President and his guests and the minimum staff necessary to serve dessert and coffee."

"Yes, sir."

"Okay, everyone," Jake finished. "Let's hope we're freaking out over nothing. Keep your heads cool, your eyes peeled, your weapons hot and your movements sharp. We've prepared for anything Trident is going to throw at us. Sound good?"

Everyone agreed as one. "Outstanding. Radio silence is in effect unless it's an urgent communication. I need to know everything that happens the instant you guys do, and I don't want you to have to shout over anyone to tell me, nor do I want to have to shout to issue any important instructions I may have."

The team leads acknowledged again, and Jake breathed deeply and focused on the situation unfolding on the screens. The SUVs drove one block past the barrier surrounding the White House, then turned inward. When they passed each other, Jake held his breath, but they just continued to the street past the barrier before turning down toward Constitution Avenue.

They were casing the defenses. Jake frowned and passed that information to his team leads. "Anyone have a license plate?"

"They're all government plates, sir. FBI."

Jake frowned. "Does the FBI have assets in the area, Jess?"

"Calling the Director now."

Jake waited a tense three minutes while Jess called. He watched as the SUVs slowly proceeded to Constitution Avenue before turning away and heading in opposite directions from the barrier.

Jess called back, her tone urgent. "No, Jake. No FBI assets in the area."

Jake nodded. "All right. Roaming units, take them down. They are not FBI, repeat, they are not FBI. Possible terrorist vehicles."

Blue dots waiting at various intersections throughout the city began to move, converging on the red dots that represented the SUVs. Jake tensed slightly, forcing himself to breathe as the Washington Police surrounded the threats. "Come on, boys," he said, "let's go nice and easy."

They didn't go nice and easy. No sooner had the red dots stopped moving on the screen when his earpiece buzzed.

"Roamer One, the terrorists have opened fire! Automatic weapons, and… shit!"

The epithet was followed by the sound of an explosion. Jake watched in horror as one of the blue dots winked out. He tapped his earpiece. "Roamer One! Come in!"

"Roamer One here," the badly shaken WPD officer replied. "Terrorists have heavy weaponry. Machine guns and RPGs. Roaming units are pulling back until SWAT can arrive."

"Roger that. RRTs One and Two proceed to the sites of the engagement. Deadly force is authorized. Terrorists have automatic weapons and RPGs, please feel free to take them out by any means you deem necessary. Air One, get my jets in the air."

Another blue dot winked out, and a moment later, a voice came over his earpiece. "Ground One, Roamer Two is KIA, repeat, Roamer Two is KIA. Request snipers. They have us pinned down at 14th street."

"Snipers, aye. Eagle Two, do you have a shot?"

"Negative Ground One. The SUVs are armored, and the terrorists are firing through holes cut in the windshield."

"How soon can you get into position?"

"It'll take at least three minutes, sir."

"Get moving. As soon as you have a shot, you take it, do you understand? Don't wait for my order."

"Understood."

"Air One, tell the jets to paint the targets and lock weapons to fire on my command. Advise them of the RPGs."

"Ground One, if they fire on those targets, we're looking at significant collateral damage."

"I realize that, Air One. That will be a last resort."

"Ground One, this is Quiver One, the hen and the chick are on the move. ETA to Delta forty minutes."

"Roger, Quiver One. What route are you taking?"

"The one that takes us as far away from the terrorist SUVs as possible."

"Outstanding. Let me know when you get there."

"Ground One, this is Roamer One. We have disabled the terrorist SUVs. RPG has gone quiet, we believe they had only a few rounds of ammo. Units twenty-seven, thirty-nine and forty-three are down, casualties unknown at this time. Terrorists are still firing, but they are down to semi-automatic rifles and handguns. Situation is in hand. We'll soften them up a bit, then we'll—"

Another explosion sounded over the radio, loud enough that Jake had to shut off his earpiece wit. He stared in horror at the screen as the four red dots disappeared, along with nine of the blue dots.

He tapped his earpiece again and said, "Someone tell me what the hell just happened?"

"Ground One, this is Air One," Peterson replied, his voice subdued. "The terrorist vehicles self-destructed. It's unknown how many casualties at this point, but the charges left craters the width of the street."

"Ground One, this is Roamer Nine. We have a building fire on our end."

Jake felt a whirlwind of emotions: grief, anger, and frustration were paramount. Trident may not have reached the President, but they were making law enforcement pay dearly for their failure.

Anger pushed grief and frustration aside and found a new target in the form of President Bryan Jackson. All this for a dinner. Hundreds of thousands of dollars to prepare, hundreds of thousands in damage, millions or more if that fire spread, and dozens dead already. For what? So Bryan could show the world that he could have his buddies over for dinner?

"Ground One, please advise."

Jake pushed his emotions to the side and said, "Jess, dispatch fire rescue to Constitution Avenue and Fourteenth Street. Roamer Nine, seal off the incident area to civilian traffic. Roamer… who's in charge on the other side?"

"Me, sir," a voice so youthful it might have been a child's answered. "Roamer, uh, Seventeen."

"Roamer Seventeen, form a perimeter as well. No one gets in or out. Air One, please advise the Air Force that their targets have elected to take the easy way out. Keep the jets in the air flying a low CAP for now. Any other sign of threats or suspicious activity?"

Jess replied to that. "No, Jake, nothing else."

She sounded defeated. It wasn't a typical tone of voice for her. She was always optimistic, no matter the situation. Yet another thing Bard had ruined.

I'm going to kill you, Bard. You and Drew.

The thought came to him as clear as crystal. His professional training told him not to think like that, but deep inside, he knew he meant it with every fiber of his being.

And when the time came, he knew he wouldn't hesitate.

"Ground One, it's RRT One."

Garrett's voice was filled with tension and mixed with a healthy dose of fear. "What is it?"

"Trident is inside the White House. They came in through the tunnels."

CHAPTER TWENTY THREE

Jake remembered his first combat action as vividly as if it took place yesterday. He was outside of a small village in Iraq on patrol with infantry. Snipers weren't ordinarily allowed on patrols because their skillset was considered too valuable to the war effort to risk, but there hadn't been any activity in that area for over a year. Jake was there on the off chance that one of the high-value targets passed through, but no one expected that to happen.

So, Jake got bored and asked permission to join a patrol. The company CO agreed, not seeing any reason to force a Marine to remain cooped up on reservation without good cause.

The patrol went smoothly up until they crested a low rise a mile and a half from the outpost. The first indication that anything was wrong came when a loud explosion rattled Jake from head to toe. The world spun around him as his vehicle was flipped by the IED, landing on its head and burning rapidly from the fuel leak the bomb had caused.

Almost immediately, Jake's senses muted. He knew he was unbuckling his belt and evacuating the vehicle. He felt himself shoulder his rifle—a standard issue M16, since this wasn't a sniper mission—and return fire to the insurgents. He heard himself shout instructions to the other members of the patrol, cutting through the panic and ensuring an organized response to the ambush.

He was aware of all of those things, but they seemed to occur outside of himself. None of it seemed real. It was as though he were walking in a dream.

That was how he felt now as he ran from the situation room toward the sounds of fighting. He could feel his feet hitting the ground, but the sensation felt muffled and dull. He could hear himself issuing commands to his team leads, but it sounded like his voice came from far away and behind a waterfall.

This was the worst-case scenario. Somehow, Trident had gotten into the White House. All of their agents and resources were for nothing.

As he made his way to the dining room, pieces of the puzzle began to connect. The SUVs were a diversion designed to pull their attention and resources away from the real objective. The threats to Sheila were meant to draw the agents in the tunnels away from Trident's point of ingress and egress. Bard had read him like a book.

No, Drew had read him like a book. This had his filthy, bloodstained hands all over it. He knew Jake, understood how he fought, and he used that knowledge to prep Bard so that Trident knew exactly how to act to ensure their operation was a success.

I'm going to kill you, Drew. I'm going to make it last a long time.

He didn't dwell on the anger. It wouldn't serve him now.

But it would serve him later.

He reached the dining room and kicked the locked door open. He was nearly skewered by a burst of rifle fire for his trouble. A shot from his service weapon put the terrorist down, and Jake was able to take stock of the situation.

It wasn't good. Trident operatives poured into the room, engaging the nearly overwhelmed Secret Service agents. The VIPS sheltered behind overturned tables, but those would offer precious little help against assault rifles. Many of the agents shielded VIPs with their bodies, as they were trained to do. Many of them perished as gunfire overwhelmed their body armor or found weak points.

So far, it appeared that while several VIPs were injured, none were killed. The President was unharmed, surrounded by Garrett's RRT. Another RRT was present in the room, and as Jake worked his way to the President, he could see that Trident's progress was quickly waning as the RRTs with their superior equipment and firepower took control of the situation.

The President met Jake's eyes, and Jake could see the fear and guilt emanating from Bryan's face.

Jake kept his own gaze cold. He would always respect the office of the Presidency, but his respect for the man had diminished considerably. Maybe he would feel differently later when he didn't have to stare at the dead bodies of his comrades, but right now, a part of Jake wouldn't have minded if one of Trident's bullets found their mark.

Fortunately, that part of himself had no impact on his actions or decision-making. He fired quickly and efficiently, taking out no fewer than eight Trident terrorists as he worked his way to the President.

His unforeseen arrival turned the tide in favor of the Secret Service. He heard a voice he didn't recognize call for the Trident terrorists to regroup outside of the dining room.

"RRT Two," Jake called over his earpiece. "Follow them and keep pressure on them. Don't let them back in here. Make this hurt! RRT One, get the President out of here. Take Route Leo. Air One, scramble

Marine One now. If they can't get here before one of your units, then that unit will become Marine One. Understood?"

Marine One was the President's helicopter and was always ready to fly. In reality, there were four different Marine Ones to ensure that one of them was always ready to go. At the moment, Jake didn't give a fuck what helicopter the President ended up on as long as he was evacuated safely.

"What about us?" a tearful Secretary of Education asked.

"House One, are you here?"

"House One is KIA, sir. This is House Three."

Jake's lips thinned. "House Three, evacuate the VIPs. Take them to the South Lawn. Air One, any helicopter not designated Marine One is to evacuate VIPs. Your unit is the only exception. Maintain top cover and coordinate with the Air Force to provide area reconnaissance. Anything moves that isn't ours, I want to know about it. Roamer Nine, is the city locked down yet?"

"Negative. All resources are focused on the situation at hand."

"If you can, lock down the city. If not, then lock down as much square footage of the area surrounding the White House as possible."

"Will do."

"Where do you want the VIPs transported?" Peterson asked.

"Andrews. Tell the Air Force to expect them, and if the Army has any Guard units that can provide security, I want them."

He didn't get a chance to hear Air One's response because a hail of gunfire sounded from the hall outside, and the lead of RRT two said through the radio. "Ground One, be advised, multiple targets inbound! At least four dozen terrorists armed with riot shields and automatic weapons!"

Dammit.

He looked around and saw RRT One retreating through the opposite hallway. "Garrett let me know when the President—"

A burst of gunfire drowned him out, and Jake saw RRT One rapidly backpedaling back into the room. The Special Agents in suits looked around wildly. This was the first time Jake had ever seen Secret Service agents panic, but he didn't blame them. He was closer to panic than he would have liked himself.

How did Trident have so many terrorists? For God's sake, they were operating at company strength just for this one attack. How could this have flown under everyone's radar for so long?

Something hit his right side and drove him to the ground. The Secret Service agent who tackled him said, “There’s at least seventy, Sir. We have nowhere to go.”

"Then we stay here," Jake said, "and we take every single one of the best—"

A red hole replaced the other agent’s left eye, and Jake swore and fired at the terrorist who shot him. The Trident operative dropped, but he was replaced with three more.

“Get the VIPs up against the back wall!” Jake shouted, not bothering with the earpiece. “Surround them and shoot everyone not wearing a Secret Service uniform!”

The agents moved quickly and efficiently. Now that they knew they had no way out, panic was replaced with resolve. If they were going to die, they were going to die well. Jake felt a rush of pride for the men and women around him. Each and every one of them had earned their badges.

He made his way close to Garrett, firing and dropping three terrorists on his way to her. The hard-as-nails RRT leader was bleeding from a shrapnel cut above her left eye, but her eyes blazed with fury as she held the Trident forces to the doorway, not allowing them any closer.

“Do you have any smokes?” Jake asked her, using RRT slang for smoke grenades.

Garrett’s eyes flicked to him, and her eyes widened when she realized where he was going with this. “We each have two,” she said.

“Good.”

A plan formed in Jake’s head. “RRT Two,” he said, using the earpiece this time so he could keep his voice low. “Can you get eyes outside and tell me which route is less saturated?”

Jess’s voice sounded in his head. “I can answer that. The hallway to your right is less saturated. I count ten bad guys remaining. You have twice that many the other way.”

“Thank you,” Jake said. “RRT One, I want your team to move forward and clear the way with the President on my mark and not an instant before or after. Agents, you will follow with the other VIPS. RRT Two, you remain behind with me and provide cover.”

Garrett and the Team Two leader acknowledged. “Jess, how are we looking outside?” Jake asked.

“Marine One has landed, and the other helicopters are orbiting awaiting their turn. The F-35s are patrolling and monitoring for sign of other terrorists. It looks clear so far.”

"Outstanding. All right, boys, girls and otherwise. On my mark."

He nodded at Garrett, and her team drew their smokes. "Three."

They pulled the pins.

"Two."

They lifted the grenades high.

"One."

They threw the grenades, and Jake saw the eyes of several Trident operatives widen as the projectiles sailed through the air.

"Mark!"

The grenades exploded, bathing the world in misty gray. The Secret Service agents and their charges headed for the hallway and out of the building. Jake and RRT Two fired at the Trident terrorists. They couldn't see if they were hitting anything. Well, Jake couldn't, anyway. The RRT agents had night-vision and infrared goggles, which might help.

Once more, time seemed to slow. With no way to see what was going on around him, Jake could only hope that RRT One and the other Special Agents had made it out with their charges.

He heard the cries of the dead and dying. Some of them were his comrades. At least one cry sounded like a VIP.

Most, however, were terrorists. Slowly, good news came filtering in. "Marine One to Ground One. We have the package. The package is received and undamaged. Repeat, the package is received and undamaged."

A cheer rose from the surviving Secret Service agents. The President had been safely evacuated. They had won. No matter what else happened today, they had done their duty.

One by one, the other VIPs were extracted. Jake and his agents continued to battle to protect them as they were evacuated. Agents continued to fall around Jake, but those who survived fought bravely. Jake felt a rush of anger at the President and his cabinet for endangering so many good men and women, but he pushed that emotion away. He could be angry about it later. Right now, he had a job to do.

Five helicopters landed and lifted off, evacuating all fifteen guests. One unit, Air Three, reported that one of the VIPs, the Secretary of the Treasury, had been critically injured, and they were diverting to George Washington University Hospital to seek treatment. Other than that, none of the VIPs suffered more than scrapes and bruises.

The smoke slowly cleared. The Trident attackers dwindled until finally there was no one left but Jake and the exhausted agents. Jake tapped his earpiece. “Okay, RRT Two. Our turn. Let’s get out of here and mop up on the way.”

Then he heard the telltale clink of a grenade skipping across the floor.

Not a smoke grenade.

His eyes widened. He opened his mouth to say, “Grenade!”

But the word never came out.

CHAPTER TWENTY FOUR

"Get up! Get up, Marine!"

Jake groaned and tried to stand but ended up falling on his face. His ears rang, and his stomach roiled with nausea. He could hear the sounds of the battle around him, the screams of the dead and dying. Soon, his screams would add to theirs.

A rough hand jerked him to his feet, and an equally rough one slapped him hard across the face. Jake gasped and stared into the eyes of his friend, Andrew McNeill. McNeill's eyes revealed just as much fear as Jake felt, but the steel behind that fear was far stronger than the fear.

"Get your shit together, Jake!" Drew shouted at him. "We are U.S. Marines, and if we die, we will do it with our knives buried in the throats of the assholes who killed us! Grab your rifle and fight!"

Drew's words galvanized Jake. He bent over and picked up his rifle. Drew nodded approvingly and clapped his friend on the shoulder. "Let's take the bastards with us!"

The two Marines shouted their war cry, rushing forward through the firefight, rifles stuttering as they rained red, white and blue death on their nation's enemies. Jake felt his fear dissipate as he ran. His name would be in the newspapers tomorrow morning, but amid the tears of grief his parents would shed would be tears of pride. Their son was a Marine.

Another bomb went off, lifting Jake off of his feet and throwing him hard to the ground. He rolled onto his hands and knees, gritting his teeth and struggling to stand.

"Get up, Marine! Now! Get up, Jake!"

"Get up, Jake!"

Jake opened his eyes. His vision swam, and he tasted blood in his mouth. His entire body felt like it was on fire. At the same time, his entire body felt immobilized as though he was glued to the ground.

"Jake, Dammit!" The voice said again. Jake recognized it as Jess "They're coming! There are more Trident agents, Jake, and they're coming! Get up!"

Jake's vision swam, and a fresh wave of nausea drove him to the brink of unconsciousness.

"Jake, for God's sake! Sheila needs you! Get your ass *up!"*

At the mention of Sheila's name, Jake opened his eyes fully. With a cry of effort, he got to his feet. Dizziness threatened to put him right back on the ground, but he gritted his teeth and then bared them.

"They want me? They can come get me."

He didn't realize he had said that out loud until Jess said, "While I appreciate the sentiment, I think it would be better for you to get them so you can then get the bomb they've hidden in the White House."

That sobered Jake instantly. "Bomb?"

"Yes. Eli Bard is on the news. It's a recorded video of him saying that when the White House explodes in five minutes, it will be a testament to the resolve of those who yearn for true freedom, yadda yadda, typical terrorist bullshit. The point is, there's a bomb, and to get to it, you need to get past the Trident agents who are—"

One of the Trident terrorists poked his head into the dining room. Jake shot him with his service weapon and rushed for the hallway.

"No!" Jess cried. "The other way. I have a path for you."

Jake pivoted on his heel and changed direction, following the route the others had taken to evacuate the building. Around him, he saw the bodies of over twenty Secret Service agents killed in the gunfight and the grenade explosion.

Their parents would shed tears of grief and pride the next morning.

He reached the hallway and shot a surprised Trident agent in between the eyes. He caught the man before he fell and took his rifle.

"Where am I going, Jess?"

"The Oval Office. The bomb was planted under the President's desk."

"During the meal?"

"That's my guess. I'm a little more concerned with how it's disabled than how it's planted, though."

A chill ran through Jake. "Okay, I'm going in. Any units on the White House grounds or nearby, please respond."

"Ground One, this is RRT Four. Boy, am I glad to hear your voice."

"Tell me all about it later, RRT Four. Right now, I need you to enter the White House and make your way to the Oval Office. Shoot anything that isn't me."

"Understood, sir. On our way."

"ETA?"

"Three minutes."

“Outstanding.”

He ran through the corridors toward the Oval Office. His heart pounded, and each step he took, he was certain he would feel the building explode around him.

He reached the office just in time to see four terrorists aiming rifles at him.

Jake didn’t slow. He sprinted into the room, feeling bullets whip behind him as the terrorists tried and failed to adjust to the blitz attack.

He took out two more terrorists as he dove behind the desk. When the other two realized he was going to reach the bomb, they rushed him, crying out in desperation.

He had time to shoot one of the operatives before the final terrorist grabbed his wrist and wrenched it hard, forcing him to drop the weapon. He reached for it with his other hand, but the terrorist kicked it away and wrenched his wrist again, forcing him to the ground.

Jake roared and tore his hand away, ignoring the soft tear he felt in his wrist when he did. He slammed his good fist into the terrorist's nose. It pulped, and the man cried out. Jake drew his knife and finished the job, burying the weapon in his assailant's throat. The man gurgled as he sank to the ground, but Jake didn't watch him die.

He ran to the desk, ignoring the shooting pains that were now moving up his right wrist to his shoulder. He tapped his earpiece, reaching around with his left. His right fingers wouldn’t close anymore.

“Jess, I’m at the bomb. I’m down to one hand. How is the situation outside the door?”

“RRT Two is engaging with the remaining terrorists in the hallway just outside of the dining room. They have the situation under control.”

“How much time to disarm this thing?”

“three minutes.”

Jake’s heart sank, but he forced his fear away. That meant three minutes to achieve victory.

He looked at the bomb, and his eyes widened. He expected a crude stack of TNT with a little clock timer on it. Instead, it was a brick of C4 large enough to destroy the entire damned building and leave nothing left but a smoking crater.

The timer was a digital egg timer counting down through seventy when Jake saw it. Ten different wires stuck out from the timer into the C4.

“Okay, Jess. Any idea where to start?”

Jess didn’t answer. Or maybe she did, but Jake didn’t hear what she said. What he heard instead was the soft click of a rifle and then a familiar voice say, "Leave that alone, Jake. You start running now, and you might make it out of the White House before it goes off."

Rage filled Jake, but he forced himself to remain calm as he turned to face Andrew McNeill, a former Corporal in the United States Marine Corps and Jake's former best friend. Drew's hair and beard had grown, and he was a tad leaner than Jake remembered, but the hands that held the rifle were as steady and relaxed as Jake remembered.

"Hello, Drew," he said softly.

Drew didn't bother to return the greeting. "I'm not kidding, Jake. That bomb is going to go off in five minutes whether you like it or not. I'm giving you a chance not to go down with it. You've already rescued the President and his cabinet. You've won. Just let us have the building. Well," he shrugged, somehow managing to do so without moving his rifle, "we're going to take the building whether you want us to or not. Out of respect for our former friendship, I'm giving you a chance not to die with it."

Jake laughed bitterly. "Some friendship. I used to think the greatest honor I could ever have was dying at your side. Now I'm looking at you, and I don't even recognize you."

Drew's eyes narrowed. "You did this to me, Jake. I was going to be a war hero. Then you had to tell the court martial that it was my idea to abandon the SEAL team, and suddenly, I'm demoted to E1 and booted out of the Corps like it didn't matter that I had fought for my country for years."

"That's not what happened. I didn't know they were going to use that against you."

"Then you're stupid, Jake. They weren't looking for the fucking truth. They were looking for a scapegoat, and you gave them one."

"How is that my fault? You can be angry at them, but I didn't do anything."

"I'm angry at them too, and just because you acted out of stupidity and not malice doesn't mean you're innocent. I've lived my life as a pariah. My parents won't talk to me. I can't go to my hometown without being spat on."

"So you betray your country? You kill innocent people?"

"No one's innocent, Jake. We all are guilty in our own different ways."

"That's a feeble fucking excuse, Drew."

"All excuses are feeble. What I just gave you is a reason. I don't care all that much if you don't like it. Now you can either get out of here, or I can shoot you and leave myself."

The rage Jake felt bubbled up and over. With a cry, he threw himself at Drew.

The suddenness of the assault shocked Drew. He hesitated a crucial half-second before firing his weapon, and that half-second gave Jake a chance to knock the rifle barrel up. The bullet buried itself in the Oval Office's reinforced ceiling.

Jake's ears rang from the sound of the rifle going off right by his ear. He felt wetness on the side of his head and wondered if he had ruptured his eardrum. Probably.

He would deal with that later. He grappled with Drew, struggling for control of the weapon. Drew snarled and twisted, throwing Jake to the ground. He aimed his rifle again, but Jake kicked it out of the way, then tackled Drew, taking him down.

Drew lifted the butt of his rifle to bring it down on Jake's head, but Jake drove his shoulder into Drew's chin, stunning him. He stood and tore the rifle from Drew's hand, then aimed it at his former friend.

"Jake!" Jess's voice sounded in his head. "The bomb!"

Jake blinked and looked down at the bomb. It counted down from ten seconds. With a cry, he dropped the rifle and rushed for the detonator.

There was no time to think it through. He simply tore the wires off one by one.

The timer counted down.

Three seconds.

Two seconds.

One.

His last thought before the world turned white was of Sheila's beautiful blue eyes and Jess's bubbly laughter.

Except it wasn't his last thought.

The world didn't turn white.

The counter read zero, but the plastic explosive remained inert.

"Holy shit," he whispered softly.

Then he remembered Drew. He turned around, expecting Drew to have his rifle aimed and ready to kill Jake, but Drew was gone. Jake felt a touch of disappointment, but in the elation of having survived and disarmed the bomb, that disappointment was mild.

"You did it! Jake, you did it! You did it, you did it, you did it!"

Jess cheered and whooped over the earpiece, and Jake smiled, the elation of success replacing his fear and temporarily relieving the pain in his injured wrist. "Well, how about that?" he said. "Looks like Bard doesn't get his big boom after all. He still on TV?"

"Yep. He's *pissed.* I guess this was live, not recorded. Ooh, you should see him, he's as red as a tomato. Oops, he's gone."

"Haha. Dumbass."

"Speaking of dumbasses, it's fuchsia, salmon and hot pink."

"What?"

"Fuchsia, salmon and hot pink. Not dark pink, medium pink and light pink. For God's sake, why do men have such trouble seeing colors? Those are three very separate colors."

"Yeah, they're pink, Jess. They're all fucking pink. Not fuchsia. And salmons only turn pink when they're about to mate."

"Well, if you ever want to mate, learn the difference between fuchsia, salmon and hot pink. I guarantee you Sheila knows."

Jake chuckled. He was about to retort when something came to him. Oh God, Sheila! "Jess, you said Sheila needed me. What's wrong? Is her evac team compromised?"

"Huh? Oh, no. I just said that because you weren't getting up. I figured if I said the name of the woman you loved, you might get your shit together. It worked!"

Jake thought he could detect a touch of emotion in Jess's voice, but before he could ask if she was okay, a voice interrupted them. "Ground One, this is Quiver One. Hen and egg are safe at Delta, repeat, we are safe at Delta. I've been listening in to the situation up top. Sounds like you have things under control."

"Ground one, this is RRT Four. Terrorist threat is neutralized, repeat, terrorist threat is neutralized!"

"Roger, RRT Four. Quiver One, you are right. We have things under control. Remain at Delta until instructed otherwise."

"Will do, Ground One. Damned good job, Mercer."

Congratulations poured in from the other team leaders. Jake grinned, but the grin slowly turned into a grimace as his adrenaline levels ebbed and the pain he felt intensified. He looked down to take stock of his injuries.

His eyes widened. The front of his uniform was soaked in blood. His body armor was riddled with chips and holes, and his legs were shredded. His right hand hung at an odd angle, and the wrist was swollen to the size of a grapefruit. An odd bulge near his elbow told him he had torn a muscle. He couldn't see his face and decided that was a good thing. How he had managed to walk and fight like this was beyond him.

"Wow," he said, "I… um…"

He felt the world spin around him, but he didn't feel himself hit the ground. As darkness took him, he could hear Jess's voice in his ear. "Jake? God, please be okay. Jake?"

EPILOGUE

"You know the difference between Marines and everyone else, Mercer?"

"No, Master Gunny Sergeant."

"Not a damned thing."

Jake blinked. Master Gunnery Sergeant Max Harrison was known for speaking cryptically, but this was easily the last thing he expected the grizzled veteran to say. "Gunny Sergeant?":

"Master Gunny Sergeant. I earned that Master, Corporal."

"Yes, Master Gunny. But..."

"Not. A. Damned. Thing. We're all humans. We have two eyes, two arms, two legs, one asshole. Well, some of the brass have a second one just underneath their nose, but for the most part, we're all the same as everyone else. We're in better shape than a lot of people, but an Olympic athlete is in better shape than we are. We can fire our rifles well, but a... well, okay, we *probably do that better than other people.*

"My point is, the only thing that makes us different; the only thing that makes it mean something when you look in the mirror and tell yourself that you're a Marine is your will. You will go where other people will stop. You will succeed where other people fail. You will win where other people lose. You will survive where other people die.

"You'll do all of those things because you're a Marine. That means jack-all in a scientific sense, but it means everything in a practical sense. You are a Marine, and God help anyone foolish enough to stand across from you. Do you understand what I mean, Mercer?"

"I do, Gunny Sergeant."

"Well, I Goddamn hope so, Corporal, because you forgot the Master again, so now you get to run a half-marathon in full gear. You have ten minutes to meet me right back here in battle dress with your loaded ruck and your rifle. If you're a second late, I'll make you carry me."

Jake couldn't stifle a grin as he ran for his ruck. He knew he would likely be throwing up his last meal by the time he finished this run, but that was okay.

He was a Marine. He would complete the run, and this was the last time he would forget to call Max Master Gunny.

"Jake?"

The voice startled Jake awake. He breathed in sharply and tried to sit, but a soft hand pressed against his chest, forcing him back down to the bed.

"Jess? Is that you? Where am I?"

"It's me, Jake," the voice repeated.

Not Jess.

"Sheila. You're here."

He reached for her, and she grabbed his hand in hers and pressed it to her chest. His vision cleared slowly, and he looked up at the smiling face of the woman he loved.

He smiled. "Hey, Sheila."

She laughed, and tears welled in her eyes. "Hey, Jake."

They sat that way for a long while, enjoying the comfort of each other's presence. They had both suffered greatly, but that was all right. That didn't matter anymore. They were safe, and they were here together.

"Where am I?"

"You're at George Washington University Hospital," Sheila replied. "Dad had you airlifted here once the terrorist threat was ended."

"Good."

He tried to sit, but she pushed him down again. "Rest," she commanded. "You'll be here another three days, at least."

"I can't be here… wait, *another* three days?"

Her smile faded slightly. "You nearly died, Jake. Your injuries were severe. Do you remember?"

The image of his shredded legs and Swiss cheesed body armor came back to mind. "Right. How bad is it?"

She shook her head and laughed. "Did you not hear me say you nearly died?"

"I mean my face. I'm still pretty, right?"

She laughed again, then leaned in close. "You're still pretty."

Her lips parted. Jake closed his eyes and prepared to receive her kiss.

He heard the door open and turned toward it to see the President walk into the room. Sheila sat up quickly, but not quickly enough. Bryan looked at his daughter, then at Jake, then back at his daughter. His expression changed to something unreadable.

Sheila lowered her head, but Jake kept his gaze steadily on Bryan's. After a moment, the President took a deep breath and said gently, "Sheila, may I have a word with Jake alone?"

Sheila nodded. She stood, but before she left, she squeezed Jake's hand. Jake watched her go, then turned to Bryan. He was surprised to see that the anger he felt toward the man before was gone. Both men had jobs to do, and as much as Jake wanted to blame him for the deaths of his comrades, he couldn't blame Bryan for wanting to show the world that the United States would not be cowed by terrorists.

"I wanted to thank you," the President said. "You made this disaster far less disastrous than it could have been. I've been talking to Art. The Secret Service has dropped the Internal Affairs case against you. You'll get to keep your job."

"Thank you, Sir. And Trident?"

"Well, pretty much every three-letter agency in the country is looking into them, and it looks like you devastated them with your defense of the White House. The leaders are still at large, but it's believed they have fewer than ten operatives with them."

Jake tried to see this as good news, but if Bard could have gotten so many to sacrifice their lives for him before, he could do it again. "We need to find them, Sir."

"And you will. You will lead the manhunt, but for now, you'll lead it from afar while you rest and recuperate." He stepped forward and laid a hand on Jake's shoulder. "You did well, Jake. Damned well."

Jake smiled. "Thank you, sir." His smile faded a moment. "Sir. You should know. Sheila and I—"

"I know," Bryan interrupted. His smile hardened slightly. "I always knew. You should keep that in mind."

He squeezed Jake's shoulder again, then left the room, leaving Jake to wonder what his reaction meant.

He settled slowly into his bed and looked up at the ceiling. Trident was defeated for now, but as long as Bard and Drew were at large, they would come back. His career was safe for now, but the bad blood between him and Art would continue to fester. He was out in the open with Sheila, but he had no idea how that would end.

He smiled softly and said to the empty room, "Having fun yet?"

NOW AVAILABLE!

ABSOLUTE DAMAGE
(A Jake Mercer Political Thriller—Book #2)

"Thriller writing at its best."
--Midwest Book Review (*Any Means Necessary*)

From the #1 bestselling and USA Today bestselling author Jack Mars (with over 10,000 five-star reviews) comes a groundbreaking new political thriller series: when the President of the United States or his family are threatened, it is up to Jake Mercer, former Marine sniper turned Secret Service agent, to protect them from dangers—both foreign and domestic.

When Paris falls prey to a ruthless bio-terrorist, Secret Service Agent Jake Mercer must race against time to prevent a deadly pandemic, and to protect world leaders—including the President of the United States.

"Thriller enthusiasts who relish the precise execution of an international thriller, but who seek the psychological depth and believability of a protagonist who simultaneously fields professional and personal life challenges, will find this a gripping story that's hard to put down."
--Midwest Book Review, Diane Donovan (regarding Any Means Necessary)

"One of the best thrillers I have read this year. The plot is intelligent and will keep you hooked from the beginning. The author did a superb job creating a set of characters who are fully developed and very much enjoyable. I can hardly wait for the sequel."
--Books and Movie Reviews, Roberto Mattos (re Any Means Necessary)

ABSOLUTE DAMAGE is the second book in a new series by #1 bestselling and critically acclaimed author Jack Mars, whose books have received over 10,000 five-star reviews and ratings. The series begins with ABSOLUTE THREAT (book #1).

A gripping and unpredictable political thriller, the Jake Mercer series is a page-turning action series that will leave you unable to put it down. This fresh and exciting action hero will have you turning pages late into the night, and fans of Brad Taylor, Vince Flynn, and Tom Clancy are sure to fall in love.

Future books in the series are also available!

Jack Mars

Jack Mars is the USA Today bestselling author of the LUKE STONE thriller series, which includes seven books. He is also the author of the new FORGING OF LUKE STONE prequel series, comprising six books; of the AGENT ZERO spy thriller series, comprising twelve books; of the TROY STARK thriller series, comprising seven books; of the SPY GAME thriller series, comprising nine books; and of the new JAKE MERCER thriller series, comprising five books (and counting).

Jack loves to hear from you, so please feel free to visit www.Jackmarsauthor.com to join the email list, receive a free book, receive free giveaways, connect on Facebook and Twitter, and stay in touch!

BOOKS BY JACK MARS

JAKE MERCER THRILLER SERIES
ABSOLUTE THREAT (Book #1)
ABSOLUTE DAMAGE (Book #2)
ABSOLUTE FORCE (Book #3)
ABSOLUTE PERIL (Book #4)
ABSOLUTE TREASON (Book #5)

THE SPY GAME
TARGET ONE (Book #1)
TARGET TWO (Book #2)
TARGET THREE (Book #3)
TARGET FOUR (Book #4)
TARGET FIVE (Book #5)
TARGET SIX (Book #6)
TARGET SEVEN (Book #7)
TARGET EIGHT (Book #8)

TROY STARK THRILLER SERIES
ROGUE FORCE (Book #1)
ROGUE COMMAND (Book #2)
ROGUE TARGET (Book #3)
ROGUE MISSION (Book #4)
ROGUE SHOT (Book #5)
ROGUE STRIKE (Book #6)
ROGUE ORDER (Book #7)

LUKE STONE THRILLER SERIES
ANY MEANS NECESSARY (Book #1)
OATH OF OFFICE (Book #2)
SITUATION ROOM (Book #3)
OPPOSE ANY FOE (Book #4)
PRESIDENT ELECT (Book #5)
OUR SACRED HONOR (Book #6)
HOUSE DIVIDED (Book #7)

FORGING OF LUKE STONE PREQUEL SERIES

PRIMARY TARGET (Book #1)
PRIMARY COMMAND (Book #2)
PRIMARY THREAT (Book #3)
PRIMARY GLORY (Book #4)
PRIMARY VALOR (Book #5)
PRIMARY DUTY (Book #6)

AN AGENT ZERO SPY THRILLER SERIES
AGENT ZERO (Book #1)
TARGET ZERO (Book #2)
HUNTING ZERO (Book #3)
TRAPPING ZERO (Book #4)
FILE ZERO (Book #5)
RECALL ZERO (Book #6)
ASSASSIN ZERO (Book #7)
DECOY ZERO (Book #8)
CHASING ZERO (Book #9)
VENGEANCE ZERO (Book #10)
ZERO ZERO (Book #11)
ABSOLUTE ZERO (Book #12)

Made in the USA
Coppell, TX
13 July 2024

34583064R00085